A WINTER WONDERLAND

REBECCA HUNTER

Christmas Whodunnit in Seaside Town's Crime of Passion
By Maddy Stein, USA Times staff writer

DELILAH'S COVE, Or. – Someone in this quiet coastal town has a mysterious way of celebrating the holidays.

It starts with an anonymous gift of a fruitcake and ends with two people falling in love.

The bunt-shaped fruitcakes began showing up in seemingly random mailboxes five years ago. There was nothing to distinguish the packaging, just a generic holiday cake tin inside a brown box with four mini bottles of Wild Turkey and a card reading: "Enjoy the magic of Christmas and prepare to fall in love." The return address was a Delilah's Cove P.O. box.

Every year since, a collection of people from the West Coast to the East Coast with no ostensible connection have received the cakes. Yet no one has been able to conclusively prove who's sending them, despite a growing list of suspects. Some have called the cakes magical, while others maintain they're a well-orchestrated publicity stunt to turn Delilah's Cove into a thriving tourist destination. After all, Delilah, the town's founder, was a suspected witch, so a love-potion fruitcake would be a fitting gimmick.

Whether a true believer or a cynic, the general consensus is that the fruitcakes have had a strange way of bringing unlikely couples together.

"I didn't think anything of it at first," said Janis Whiting, who received the cake two years ago in Coeur d'Alene, Idaho. "It was Christmastime, and I figured my company had sent it. Then I saw something on the news about people receiving a mysterious fruitcake from a Christmas cupid in Oregon, dug up the box, and sure enough, it was from Delilah's Cove. Crazy, right?"

Whiting, 32, said she has never been to the seaside town, nor does she know anyone from Delilah's Cove, but believes the cake was part of her destiny.

"I'd just gone through a bad breakup, and out of nowhere, I get the package. Then my old high-school boyfriend calls, says he just moved to Coeur d'Alene and decided to look me up. Boom, four months later, we're engaged."

Hattie Reed, the postmaster in Delilah's Cove, said that first Christmas and every one since, she's gotten calls from recipients requesting to know who sent the fruitcakes.

"I have my suspicions," she said, but stopped short of naming names. "I started logging the calls and so far, twenty-five people have reported receiving the fruitcakes and falling in love, just like the note said. My husband thinks it's a load of hooey, but you can't argue with those numbers."

Over at Delilah's Cut and Curl, the salon staff and clients were divided.

"Someone at the chamber of commerce cooked this up," said Darla Jensen, one of the stylists. "I call it the power of suggestion. You tell someone the cake will make you fall in love, and the next thing you know, you're in love."

There was much debate, but all agreed that the news stories had given the town a certain degree of cache.

Mayor Randy Kim admits that the lore of the fruitcakes has indeed put Delilah's Cove on the map but denies that they're the brainchild of an elaborate marketing scheme.

"I'm just as flummoxed as everyone else," he said. "And honestly, I don't think we would've gone with fruitcakes as a symbol of the city. People usually throw them away or regift them, not exactly the image we want to portray."

At the sole bakery in town, Dani Cornfield was ready to dish.

"I know a lot of folks think it's me," she said. "But wouldn't that be a little too obvious? Come on."

Cornfield said she has narrowed it down to three possible culprits: Bruce Willows, Tuff McNeil or the church ladies. Willows loves his romance novels, she said. McNeil owns the diner and is a direct descent of Delilah.

"For all we know, he's a witch, too," Cornfield said. "And even if he isn't, it's a boon to his cash register."

And the church ladies? Cornfield didn't have a good reason except "they always have their noses in everyone else's business."

Willows and McNeil denied being involved, and the church ladies could not be reached for comment.

"I just wish someone would send me one of those cakes," Cornfield said. "I haven't had a date in two years."

*

CHAPTER ONE

Selena pulled her ailing car onto the shoulder of the road and rolled to a stop. The car gave another ominous rattle, this one louder than the last. Tendrils of smoke seeped out from one side of the hood, then the other. *Shit*. She turned off the engine and rested her head on the steering wheel.

On both sides, the pine forest rose up, thick and dense, making a little valley for this stretch of the two-lane road. She couldn't be more than ten or fifteen miles from her house, but it was too far to walk in this weather. Especially considering her shoe selection. The bright red ballerina slippers had been perfect for a quick trip back to Boston for Melanie's holiday party…but not nearly as suitable for a walk in the blustery rain of Upstate New York.

Plus, walking home would take her straight through Sacred Harbor. Right past Wilkinson's Garage. And coming face to face with Jace Wilkinson would be nothing short of a disaster.

Outside her fogging windshield, the road

stretched along the deep green forest and disappeared into the mist. No other cars were in sight, not a sign of civilization. And only one mechanic shop within a fifty-mile range. She knew the number to that garage by heart, even now, nine years later. Not that she was counting.

Selena sighed. She had to call someone. The car wasn't going to fix itself, and weather along the Lake Ontario coast was notoriously unpredictable. Rain could quickly turn into ice, then feet of snow, so waiting out the storm in her broken-down car wasn't an option. If she didn't dial that familiar number, who else could she call? Her parents had moved back to Mexico long ago, and her closest high school friends had fled their hometown after graduation, just like she did. Everyone she was close to was gone. Or related to Jace.

The old, familiar ache of regrets and wants and *what ifs* churned deep in her gut, the same way it did every time memories of him crept back into her thoughts.

The way he used to smile at her.

The way he used to slip his hands under the hem of her shirt when he held her, his fingers warm against her skin.

What if he answered the phone?

Selena bit her lip. Last she'd heard, people were crossing state borders to get Jace Wilkinson to restore their antique Mercedes Benzes. He'd taken his father's garage and made it into something bigger, just as he had planned nine years ago. It was bad enough just to drive through Sacred Harbor and see the name Wilkinson on that sign. Every time she passed it, leftover memories settled in the pit of her stomach, churning.

But some poor young kid was probably stuck on Sunday tow truck duty, not Jace. And that gave her courage.

Selena looked out the window into the endless pine forest and shivered. The sky was darkening. The sun was probably nearing the horizon behind all of those storm clouds, and the car was getting colder by the minute. There was no good way to avoid what she had to do. She blew out a breath, pulled her phone out of her purse, and punched in the number.

Nothing happened.

She tried again. Still nothing. Selena studied the screen. No signal. Of course. People came to the Lake Ontario coast for wilderness, not guaranteed cell phone coverage.

Selena blew out a breath and turned to look out the rear window. The bridge over the river was still in sight. Which meant a break in the hills that lined this stretch of the coast. It was either backtrack to that bridge—on the chance that the opening meant cell phone coverage—or walk another ten miles home.

She zipped up her jacket, threw the hood over her head, and stuffed the phone in her pocket. Grabbing her keys, Selena pulled on the handle of the door. A gust of rain blew in, and the wind slammed it closed. She tried again, leaning against the door to wedge it open, then slipped out before it blew shut again. It was definitely still pouring.

She jogged along the shoulder of the road, dodging puddles and larger stones as the raindrops echoed loudly under her hood. Water pounded at her back, soaking through her designer coat, versatile for *any vacation*, according to the tag. Clearly, the designer hadn't had the pelting rain of Upstate New York in mind.

By the time Selena reached the bridge, the rain had turned to sleet, and she was shivering in fits. Her shoes were sticky and soaked, stretched a size or two larger, and her back was half-numbed. Apparently, "water resistant" was a slippery term in the raincoat industry. She pulled out her phone and huddled over it, zeroing in on the corner of the screen.

Thank God. Coverage.

Selena dialed the familiar number from her past with a shaky finger and pressed *call*. The wind roared in her ears, and her teeth chattered as she waited. Three rings. Four rings. Finally, a voice came through above the din.

"Wilkinson's Garage. How can I help you?"

Jace. It was him. Her breath caught in the back of her throat, and she squeezed her eyes shut. If she spoke, there was no turning back.

CHAPTER TWO

"Hello? Are you there?"

Jace Wilkinson glanced at the garage's phone. Someone was on the line, but he couldn't hear worth shit because of a raspy static, probably wind. He considered hanging up, but it was raining and cold as hell outside right now. Exactly the reason he had kept the line open today while he was working, even though he had given his on-call driver the day off.

He tried again. "Can I help you?"

"I n-n-need a t-t-t-t-tow."

The voice was mostly lost in the wind.

"Where are you?"

"Heading n-n-n-n-north on Lakeside Road, j-j-j-j-ust past Willow River."

Something about that voice sent a familiar prickle down his spine. It was hard to hear, but… He frowned, focusing on the call.

"What kind of car?"

"Red Mercedes."

Jace froze. There were just over eight hundred

people in Sacred Harbor and another few hundred spread out along the surrounding coast. Only one of them owned a red Mercedes. Though he had never seen it up close in his garage, he knew as well as the rest of the town did that the red Mercedes belonged to Selena Guerrero. Or Selena Miller, as she now was called. Not that he was keeping track.

"Hello? Are you s-s-s-still there?" Her voice sent another prickle down his spine, but this time, it didn't stop there.

Her voice. Goddamn. It had been so long.

"Yes, Selena," he finally said. "I'm here. I'll be there in ten."

He hung up the phone and massaged his temples. When Selena and her rich-ass husband had bought a vacation house just outside Sacred Harbor, every one of his siblings had found a way to mention it. Who the hell had the money for a vacation house, especially one they almost never visited since Selena's parents moved back to Mexico. Not that he was keeping track. It wasn't his business, not anymore. And it shouldn't matter that his sister Lizzie had mentioned seeing her at a distance during the fall. He had expected to run into her at some point, but he wasn't ready for it right now, when he had just closed up shop and changed for his brother's engagement dinner. He ran a hand through his hair. *Just get this encounter over with and move on.*

Jace grabbed his coat and jogged to the truck, the rain smacking hard against the dress pants he had just put on. Too late to change back. He jumped in and steered the truck toward the highway, the phone conversation looping through his mind.

Since Lizzie had dropped hints about Selena, he'd had some late-night fantasies that started this way. She would call for a tow, and he'd take the job instead of his regular crew. She'd be surprised to see him, the good kind of surprised. She'd tell him that she'd made a mistake all those years ago, that she shouldn't have turned him down, and he'd tell her that she could show him how sorry she was. She'd climb in, straddle him, and they'd be right back where they were nine years ago, going at it in his truck, despite her marriage. Then, after he made her feel good one more time, the way he used to—after he'd given her one last reminder of what she had given up when she traded him in for a luxury model—he'd finally put her out of his mind forever.

The cheating aspect of that scenario didn't feel great, but the fantasy always got the job done quickly.

Except this wasn't one of his fantasies. She had called him in the middle of a storm, and her teeth had been chattering. Forbidden reunion sex wasn't nearly as appealing when real-life Selena was in distress.

The wind had muffled her voice throughout the call. Why the hell was she outside? Was her husband with her, or was she alone? Jace had tried to block out all the rumors around town about why she was in Sacred Harbor a lot more often these days.

The sleet turned to hail as he neared Willow River, and he slowed the truck, searching for the red car. It was a good choice of colors, considering the situation. The car came into sight just past the bridge. Jace swung the truck around and parked. He turned off the engine and blew out a long breath. His heart was racing, as if it still hadn't gotten the message that it was better not to think about the good parts. The way she looked at him when his hands were on her bare skin. The way she loved Lizzie, too. The way she had so deftly navigated his mother, a feat most of his family still hadn't mastered. The way holding her had felt like the home he didn't know he was missing.

Jace scrubbed his hands over his face and let out a breath. It was time to get this over with.

He pulled the hood of his raincoat over his head and climbed out of the truck. The windows of the car were steamed up, and the hail piled on her windshield. He knocked on the driver's side door, and she pushed it open. Bending down, he peered in.

Selena was wrapped in a white raincoat with grey and black designs, hood up. The coat looked expensive and impractical as hell. How fitting for this new version of her. Even her raincoat said *I don't belong with a small-town guy who runs a garage.*

Big brown eyes with long, dark lashes blinked up at him, and his heart stuttered in his chest.

"J-J-J-J-Jace?" she said, her teeth knocking together. "I didn't mean to call you."

16

Despite everything, he had to laugh. "Next time, try a different number."

Selena rolled her eyes. "You know what I mean."

Yes, he did. Jace looked inside her car again and found it empty. Good. It was probably easier for both of them this way, without her husband. Seeing Selena again shouldn't be a big deal, but his heart was doing funny things in his chest.

"Come climb into the truck," he said, trying to keep his voice casual. "It's warmer in there."

She gave a quick nod and stepped out into the rain.

Jace fought images of that X-rated scenario he had imagined as he followed her. Not happening. Eighteen-year-old Selena would have been a different story. But twenty-seven-year-old Selena, in her designer coat? Not a chance in hell.

He led the way to the passenger's side and opened the door, helping her in as water poured over the hood of his raincoat. His gut clenched as her cold hand brushed against his. Damn. She was freezing, and his mind was in the gutter.

He walked around to the driver's side and climbed in, trying hard not to look at her. The engine purred, and he turned up the heaters. Well…just one good look wouldn't hurt, would it? He turned as Selena slid off her hood and lifted her hands to the truck's little heating vent, rubbing them together. Wet strands of hair fell in her face, and she pushed them away. Her hair was different.

"Your hair is brown," he said.

She smiled a little. "Y-y-you're just noticing that now?"

Jace bit back a smirk. He remembered every single inch of this woman. Intimately.

"I mean you don't have those red streaks anymore," he said. He fingered the ends of one of the strands, then let it go.

"Oh, that." She wrinkled her forehead. "I got rid of those in business school."

He studied her more closely. Those red streaks had said a lot about the girl he loved back in high school, not the woman sitting next to him. One more reminder that he didn't know her anymore, not really.

Selena shifted closer to the little vents, where streams of warm air poured out. "D-d-d-d-damn, it's cold."

Oh, right. "You should ask Santa for a new raincoat."

"Not sure how nice I've been this year," she said dryly.

He could list a dozen things about her that were nice, things he really shouldn't be thinking about right now.

"You're too wet to get warm," he said, frowning. "You need to take off some of your clothes. Jacket and shirt if they're soaked."

She gave a little snort of laughter. "Just like old times, right?"

"Not what I meant," he said, but a smile was tugging at his lips.

He really hadn't meant it that way, but now that she'd mentioned it, his mind went straight back to that well-worn scenario he liked best. *Shut it down, buddy. Not happening.*

Jace rummaged around in the bin behind his seat until he found an emergency blanket. When he turned around, she had shed her fancy shell of a jacket. Her white shirt was soaked, and he could see straight through it to her bra. Which was also bordering on transparent. *Shit.* He turned away as a rush of desire pulsed through him. Just like old times.

"I won't look," he said, pushing the blanket in her direction.

Selena shuffled around for a bit, her soft breaths echoing in the little cab, while Jace tried hard not to think about the naked woman next to him. Or the sound of her.

Don't look. She wanted something more than a high school quarterback who restores vintage cars. Don't look.

"Don't look at what?"

Jace froze. Damn. Had he said that aloud? "Uhh...nothing."

"I'm decent now, so *you* can look."

When he turned back, the blanket was wrapped tightly around her, but Selena was still shivering.

"So," she said. "Here we are again."

She let out a laugh, but the chatter of her teeth made it sound closer to a hiccup.

"Yeah. Here we are," he echoed softly. "You gonna be okay?"

She nodded.

Hell, she looked so cold. He wanted to reach across the seats to rub her arms a little, warm her up, but he resisted. There were boundaries between them. So many years between them. But how good it would feel to forget that for a while…

It was getting hot on his side of the truck. Jace unzipped the top of his coat and loosened the too-tight collar of his shirt.

"Your car broke down?" he asked. It was a stupid question, but it got his mind back to the present.

"Great way to start off the holiday season, right?" She smiled and let her eyes settle lower, on his tie. "Nice outfit. You usually rescue cars in that?"

"Only when it's a Mercedes."

Selena gave him a swat on his arm as the corners of her mouth turned up. She tucked a wisp of her hair behind her ear and brushed a drip of water off her face. Goddamn, she was beautiful. All these years of memories hadn't done her justice. Selena's full lips were red and wet from the rain, her eyes, dewy and deep brown. But she looked tired, maybe even weary.

Jace hadn't realized he was staring at her until she looked up at him again. Her eyes widened, and she looked away.

"Where's your husband?"

Selena frowned, and her brow furrowed, as if she didn't understand what he was getting at.

"I mean who will pick you up from the garage?" he added quickly. "Is your husband on his way?"

He was trying like hell to make his voice sound casual, as if her husband—the man she had lived with, kissed, lay with every night—as if he wasn't the last thing in the world Jace wanted to know about.

Selena shook her head, and her cheeks flushed a little, despite the cold. "He's my ex-husband. And I think he's in Hawaii by now with his new girlfriend and her kids."

Jace's heart gave a hard thump. So it *was* true. She wasn't married anymore. Jace cringed at the selfish pleasure he got from this news. Selena probably was hurting from this.

"I'm sorry," he said after a pause.

"I'm not," she said flatly. "Not really. I'm the one who left him."

But her mouth turned down anyway. If Jace's oldest brother Drake was right, divorces were always complicated. Not that Jace knew anything about marriage, but Selena wouldn't have made the decision lightly. Did she regret leaving her ex? He studied her for clues, but it was a lost cause. On the up side, her teeth had stopped chattering.

"I can drop you off anywhere," he said. "I'll

take your car into the shop, but the lead technician is off until Monday."

"I was heading for…for my house." She said the words slowly, like she was still getting used to the idea. "In that new development north of Sacred Harbor. If that's not too far."

He knew exactly where the house was. He had even driven by it once, years ago. But it was the words she had used that had given him pause. *My house.* Was she really living here full-time, just a few miles from him?

Still, the details didn't matter. Selena had married someone else, and he'd had his share of girlfriends and variations of that. He had made a good life for himself, taking over the family business and growing to become the most well-known Mercedes restoration shop in the Northeast. Nine years was a lifetime ago, and he hadn't thought about her in a long time…aside from the occasional sex fantasy.

Jace swiped a hand over his face. Years ago, they had been so close, so it was natural to be curious about her, wasn't it? As for the attraction, well, he could think about that later. When she wasn't sitting right next to him, with those red lips… Damn, he was thinking about kissing again.

Jace flipped up his hood and grabbed the door handle. "I'll go take care of your car."

CHAPTER THREE

Sleet pounded against the windshield as they drove up the highway, a welcome distraction. Jace could focus all his energy on the road instead of staring at Selena. The cab of the truck was damp and warm, and he glanced at her a couple times, just to make sure she wasn't shivering too badly. Between the blanket and the air blasting from the heaters, she wasn't shaking anymore, but, stripped of her fancy coat, she looked more…vulnerable. His breath caught in his throat, and he searched for something to say, something to distract himself from this closeness.

"I tried to start your car, and it didn't sound good," he said. "Just so you know, it might need some work."

"I'm hoping for a miracle fix," said Selena. "I can't afford a lot of work right now."

Jace gave her a skeptical glance, then returned his gaze to the road. "You're driving a Mercedes. Maybe our definitions of affordable are a little different."

Selena frowned at him. "That was harsh."

It was.

He sighed. "You're right. But between your car and your address, it's hard to imagine that a few thousand dollars would be too much of a stretch."

He looked over at her in time to catch an eye roll.

"Not that it's any of your business, *Jace*," she said, slowing at his name, "but I got the car and the house in the divorce. Since they're both paid off, they're actually my cheapest options. As long as both of them hold up."

"I see," he said softly. "Sorry."

But now he had more questions reeling through his mind. What was her plan, if she didn't have enough for car repairs? Where did she work? Certainly not in town. No one would have let him miss that detail. But these were more intimate questions, and most of them were way out of line. Instead, he searched for a less personal conversation topic.

"You're living up here again?"

"For now," she said. "It was just supposed to be a month or two, but…"

He waited for the end of that sentence, but it never came. Jace frowned. It didn't matter because the message behind it was clear: Selena wasn't here to stay. And there was no good reason that should bother him. He swallowed. "I see."

The rain pounded on the windshield as they

slowed through Sacred Harbor in silence. Past their high school. Past his garage. Past the well-worn turn-off to the beach. He stole glances at her a few times and found her watching as the settings of their history together played out through the window.

"How's your family?" she finally asked. Her voice was a little wary, as if she, too, was navigating these rocky waters of their past with care.

"Crazy as ever." Reluctantly, the corners of his mouth tugged up. "I'm heading to Andrew's after this for a family dinner—that's the reason for the tie. Andrew got engaged at Thanksgiving."

"Give him my best." She smiled a little. "How's the garage? You and your dad had lots of plans."

He nodded slowly as he decided how much to say. "We started on some of them, mostly the car restoration business, but…" It was hard to say the last part aloud. Still, fresh off her divorce, she probably understood that life didn't always go as planned, so he took a deep breath and pushed on. "A year ago, my dad had a stroke. So that put a lot of our ideas on hold."

"Oh, Jace."

It was her voice that caught him off guard, so full of warmth and tenderness. He had forgotten this part, the way it felt when he told her something serious, like she took some of his sadness and let it sit inside her instead.

So he didn't try to shut down the sadness, not

yet. All those plans he and his father had made came to a grinding halt the moment his father was rushed to the hospital. Most jobs in a garage required able-bodied workers, and even after his father had recovered some of the movement on his left side, keeping him on the payroll was taking accounting magic. Jace had Lizzie to thank for that magic, but still, things were tight.

The quiet settled again, a little less tense now that they were driving out of town.

"Turn here," she said after they had gone a few more miles. She pointed at the sign for the high-end development, but he already knew where to go. He slowed as they headed toward the ocean and turned down the last street that stretched out parallel to the beach. "The fourth house on the right."

The sleet had mostly let up, but dark clouds hovered ominously. Her house was completely dark. In fact, most of the neighborhood was dark. He pulled onto the sandy driveway and parked.

"You have lights here, don't you?"

"Naah, I'm living off the grid."

He jerked his head around, but she was smiling at him.

"Of course, I do." She smirked. "The security lights will come on when I walk up the driveway."

He frowned.

"I'll walk you up," he said and climbed out before she could protest. He opened her door and took the wet clothes and the handbag out of her hands as she slid off the seat, clutching the blanket around her. Her red shoes were covered with mud and sand, and her back was hunched against the cold as she headed up the front porch steps.

The house was a modern-looking structure, the kind that probably had high ceilings and all-white walls—pretty much the opposite of his house. She came to a stop in front of the door, and he held out her handbag. She unzipped it and pulled out the keys.

"Sorry if I made you late for the engagement party," she said, unlocking the door.

He shrugged. "They'll wait for me."

The door swung open into a dark hallway.

"Thanks again," she said. "I mean, I know it's your garage, but you could have hung up on me. Left me alone to walk."

He raised an eyebrow. "I considered it."

"I bet you did." She laughed a little.

Then she glanced into the house, and her smile slipped. Jace followed her gaze. The place was dark, and she was walking into it alone. The whole time he had been thinking about the past, but she was going home to a dark, empty house. Of course, she'd frowned back in the cab of his truck when she'd mentioned her ex-husband's plans. He was in Hawaii with his new girlfriend, and she was on her own.

"You gonna be okay here without a car?" he asked softly. "You have food?"

She shrugged. "Cocktail sausages, a bottle of wine. And the Harbor Café is just down the street if I get desperate. I should last for a few days."

The corners of his mouth tugged up.

"And I have plenty of work to do," she added, a smile curving on those beautiful lips.

Her eyes were somehow bright and sad at the same time, and he couldn't stop staring at her. They stood in silence in her little hallway, the muted staccato of water dripping on the porch in the background.

Just seeing her again was doing funny things to Jace's insides. He was hanging onto her every word, and he couldn't decide whether he loved it or hated it. Some of both. It was a strange feeling to have her so close again but out of reach. Still, he didn't want this moment to end. He wasn't ready to say goodbye, not yet. Just a few more minutes, and then he'd leave.

"What kind of work do you do?"

"Pretty much anything art-related that I can find," she said "I have a couple contracts for greeting cards."

He blinked in surprise. Making greeting cards was a real job? Stupid question. Of course, it was. But this was *her* job? Then the connection clicked. The birthday cards she used to make. He had saved a couple of his, together with the ring, in a box in his attic...which he sure as hell wasn't going to bring up right now. He searched for a less loaded response. "My mother still has a birthday card you made for her framed in her room."

Selena's eyes lit up. "The one of her cat?"

Jace nodded.

"Wow. I'm flattered, especially since she sort-of hated me at the end." Her smile fell a little.

His mother wasn't the easiest person under any circumstances, but it had gotten worse when she had seen the end of Selena and his relationship coming—long before he had come to terms with it. She had tried to warn him, but Jace had stubbornly believed that Selena might love him enough to stay. Lesson learned.

"It was a long time ago," he said quietly.

Selena blinked a couple times.

"Say hello to her for me." Her brow furrowed a little. "Actually, that's probably not a good idea."

He had never told his mother the story of how he'd so stupidly proposed to Selena on graduation night, but she had gotten the gist of what had happened anyway. And she still hadn't forgiven Selena for disappearing afterwards.

"You sure you're okay here?" he asked. "I can take you somewhere else if you want. Somewhere closer to town."

As soon as his words came out, he regretted them. There were places he wouldn't take her. She might have a boyfriend, and the last thing he wanted to do today was shuttle her to some other man's bed. *Happy fucking holidays, Jace.*

But she shook her head.

"I know it looks like a setting for a B horror

film." She gestured at the dark house with a flick of her wrist, and the corners of her mouth kicked up into a little smile. "But I like being on my own. I'm building my career, and it's around work that I love. I'm going to appreciate the shit out of my empty house today." Her smile grew. "And then there's the cocktail sausages. Really, I'm fine."

She put her hand on his arm, the way she used to. And in that moment, Jace slipped back in time. Alone together. They were always looking for ways to be alone. How many times had she touched him this way? Her hand slipped up his bicep. Even through his raincoat, the gesture sent bolts of heat to places they really shouldn't go right now. Her big brown eyes softened, like she was remembering, too. Was she grasping at this moment just as tightly as he was, trying not to let it go?

Lord, he missed the way she looked at him. Her eyelashes fluttered, like they used to when he was about to kiss her. So he put every hesitation aside and gave in to the overwhelming temptation.

He bent down and brushed his lips over hers. Soft. Familiar. The weight of nine years loomed, ready to push them apart, but long-buried memories were taking hold. Her breath stuttered as she stilled, just touching. The dam of memories crumbled, flooding every inch of his body, the moment she pressed her warm mouth against his. He lifted his hand to her cheek and stroked her soft skin, closing his eyes, letting himself just feel. His other hand found its way into her hair, thick and damp, and he moved his thumb gently up and down. *Selena*.

She leaned closer and caught his bottom lip between hers. *Yes*, she silently told him, *yes*. She tilted her head and opened her lips, and they were there again, back where they were years ago, kissing. It was a slow kiss, filled with new questions instead of answers.

What is this connection between us?
Have too many storms battered that bridge?

But they were kissing again, and he'd take whatever this was. It could be the last time he saw her for another ten years…or more.

That was enough to make him pull away. Jace gave himself a little shake and stepped back. How the *hell* did they get here so fast? Her eyes, heavy with desire, were focused on his lips. Once upon a time, this look would have led to more touching, more of her soft, sweet body against his. Under his.

Hell, if he didn't get out of here soon, he was going to want to do that again tonight. Which definitely wasn't a good idea. He was not going to let Selena back into his head. Not even if she was stuck in the storm alone in an empty house.

Jace took a step back. "I think I should go right now. For both of our sake."

She smiled a little. "Thanks for not leaving me on the roadside."

CHAPTER FOUR

Selena closed the front door and sagged back against it, her heart thumping hard and fast. She touched her swollen lips. It was a good thing she stayed away from Jace since she moved back in Sacred Harbor because, apparently, she was just one tow truck ride away from kissing him senseless.

Oh, Lord, he looked good after all these years. Selena hadn't let herself think about him, really think about him, in so long. His face had changed a little, his jaw sharper, his scruff darker, but so much of him had felt familiar as he drove her home. And then, when he looked down at her in the hallway, so damn sexy with his hair wet from the rain...

She would have probably invited him in for more if Jace hadn't had the sense to back away. Would it have been so bad if she did? Selena sighed and dropped her hand to her side. She'd answer that question when she wasn't so hopped up on hormones. Right now, her brain was a mess of longing and desire. And memories.

She hadn't forgotten anything. Not those Sunday brunches with his larger-than-life family. Not the stops at the beach when he'd drive her home. Not the ring he had shocked her with graduation night, his last attempt to keep her in Sacred Harbor. And she hadn't forgotten any of the reasons why turning him down had been so hard.

Shifting the blanket that covered her, she gathered her wet hair and twisted it into a knot. Yes, she had kissed Jace, and yes, it was even better than she remembered. But that didn't bring in a paycheck, nor did it sort out her future. So it was time to put him out of her mind.

Selena peeled off her wet shoes and rubbed at the red dye that had bled onto her toes. A very tempting method for warming up had just driven away, so she'd have to settle for a hot shower. Then she'd call Melanie, eat some cocktail sausages, work on a painting for a couple hours, and unwrap the packages she had picked up at—

Shit. She had left the packages in the back seat of her car, which was currently heading to Wilkinson's Garage on the back of Jace's tow truck. And her suitcase was in the trunk, too. More evidence that just being close to Jace turned off all practical thoughts. She hadn't even thought to empty her car.

Darren and Alison had set aside three packages that had come to her former apartment: one from her parents, one from Darren's sister, very thoughtful, considering the state of her and Darren's relationship, and one she didn't recognize. But Selena definitely wasn't going to call Jace and ask for them. Hopefully her car would be done by Christmas so she'd have at least one present to open this year.

The wood under her feet was cold as she started up the steps to the main floor. The last of daylight filtered in through the large windows that faced the lake, but enormous clouds hovering over the water blocked out the sunset, dark and threatening. It was going to storm again soon, maybe even snow.

Selena padded over to the far corner of the room and plugged in the little white lights that she had strung over the windows. They were her main efforts to bring in a little Christmas to this oversized house. The room lit up, soft and warm. She found the remote on the coffee table and turned on the gas flames to a slow burn. Much better. The plush U-shaped couch with its oversized pillows was inviting, but her hands were still shaking from the cold.

Clutching Jace's blanket tighter, she hobbled back to the bedroom. *Her* bedroom. She had only planned to come back to Sacred Harbor for a month or two, spend a few months in the debt-free house she now owned, licking her wounds from her divorce while she figured out what the hell came next. She had considered giving up the house and the car, hating Darren's lawyer's insinuation that she had married for money. Truthfully, she could have made a lot of it on her own at a graphic design firm if she hadn't agreed to all of Darren's work moves. Still, her lawyer had convinced her that she needed somewhere to live while she got back on her feet, even if she turned down the monthly alimony. Though Darren never had any interest in a beach house just north of her hometown, he'd fought hard to keep both residences in the split. So she had followed her lawyer's advice, and, luckily, the judge didn't give him everything he wanted, or she'd be in a bad place right now.

Instead, she owned a beautiful house on the Lake Ontario beach and had a college degree to her name, a life straight out of her parents' dreams when they'd come to this country. Minus the divorce, of course. She had no loans and low living costs, both important, considering it was hard to make a livable single income as an artist. But for now, it was her best option. If money got too tight, she could always go back to waiting tables.

The heated floor in the master bathroom was heavenly. Selena turned on the shower and let the steam fill the room. Stepping in, she moaned as the hot water splashed on her head, burning her icy fingers and toes. She tipped her head back and let the water run down her body, thawing all the other places the rain and cold had penetrated. Ohh, she never wanted to leave this cozy little shower stall.

She *could* stay here all day, or at least until the hot water ran out. No one was waiting for her to make dinner or pick up the dry cleaning. There was no rush to get to the next thing on Darren's calendar. She could even spend the day dying back those red streaks that Darren had suggested cutting out when he'd been promoted. Apparently, they didn't say *wife of a CFO*. How many other parts of herself had she quietly surrendered? What he'd really wanted was a personal assistant with benefits. And even the benefits part had waned.

At first, Selena had a hard time believing that Darren had gotten together with Alison, his real-life administrative assistant, after the divorce. Too cliché. Alison, with her subdued sweater sets and her neat blond ponytail. But that was fine with Selena, or it had been until two days ago. Until she'd walked into her old Boston apartment to pick up the packages waiting for her there and had a little conversation with said administrative assistant. Who had kids from a previous marriage. *Kids.* Darren had been adamantly against having a baby at this stage of their lives, but according to Alison, he was "such a devoted dad." In fact, Darren had even decided to switch jobs because all his traveling would be hard on her kids.

It was that last detail that Selena couldn't digest. It was still twisting in her gut, days later, bringing up the leftover bile from years' worth of moves and sacrifices and arguments about this subject. He had voluntarily stopped traveling for Alison's children, but he wouldn't do it for her, even when she'd begged him?

Happy holidays, Selena. She had spent too much of her trip to Boston dwelling on those details with Melanie, her college roommate. Time to move on.

Selena turned off the shower and wrapped herself in an enormous, fluffy towel. The divorce had been a reset button, and she had spent a lot of time in recent months doing whatever she wanted, whenever the hell she wanted to do it. Freeing, really. More recently, a bit of loneliness had set in, along with the looming question, *what comes next*? But after that kiss tonight sent her back nine years, Selena's thoughts were somewhere else. Maybe it wasn't just Jace she had left in Sacred Harbor. What parts of herself had she given up, too?

She twisted her hair into another towel and headed for her closet to put together her grand enjoying-the-day-alone ensemble. It should be tacky, the anti-Darren of outfits. The kind the wife of a CFO wouldn't wear. The kind that Alison wouldn't touch.

Selena reached for the thick, reindeer-themed leggings that Melanie had given her for Christmas a few years ago and tugged them on, the soft cotton warming her legs. Next, she went for her t-shirt drawer. She had been collecting good ones for years, snarky, campy or just plain fun. Was a holiday-themed selection the right mood? Selena sifted through t-shirts, passing by one with a Santa hat and the words *Naughty. Definitely naughty,* and settling on an old favorite, soft and dark blue, with the lines, *Of course I talk to myself. Sometimes I need expert advice*, written in white script. Darren especially hated that one.

She pulled her Boston University sweatshirt over the shirt and rummaged through her sock drawer for the warmest pair. One fluffy Christmas-themed sock stuck out. Where was the other one? No amount of searching turned it up, but who said socks had to match? Selena grabbed a grey wool sock and slipped the un-pair onto her feet.

Tacky outfit? Check.

Time for a pick-me-up call to Melanie while making a decidedly unmarried meal. Mac and cheese from a box with a cup of hot coffee. And cocktail sausages, of course. Perfect. Selena filled a pot with water, turned on the stove, and dialed her friend's number. Mel answered on the first ring.

"Hey, girl. You home yet? I saw the weather in your area wasn't looking good."

"Just got home, and the rain is turned to sleet."

"One more reason to come back to Boston. The weather is better."

Selena rolled her eyes. "Marginally."

Melanie was exactly what she needed right now. Selena had stayed in her spare bedroom as the divorce unfolded, so her friend knew all the details about Darren and her break-up. And back in college, Mel had learned more about her break-up with Jace than she probably ever wanted to know. Now that Selena was back in Sacred Harbor, Mel's advice was the old cliché about getting over the last guy by getting under someone new. Or new-ish, meaning Jace. Which meant she would be thrilled to hear about the evening's developments.

"So…my car broke down just south of Sacred Harbor."

"Did you plan that?"

Selena sent her friend a long-distance glare. "Hell, no."

Mel gave a snort of laughter. "Is this story going in the direction I think it is?"

"Depends on how dirty your mind is right now."

"I'm giving you a long-distance high five." Her friend paused. "But you two didn't get together, did you? Either that, or he's pretty quick, which means I should probably take back the high five."

Selena chuckled as she poured the box of macaroni into the boiling water. "It didn't happen. But we did kiss."

"Good start. How was it?"

"Still hot. But attraction was never the problem with us."

The problem was everything else. He had been a big distraction back in high school, crashing into each thought with his body and his sweet smile and the unmistakable desire so alive in his gaze. None of that had changed, even after all these years. And that kiss. How had she managed to block out the feeling of kissing him for all these years?

Selena poured the pasta into a colander,

juggling her phone. "I'll let you know if anything develops. And thanks again for the weekend."

"Anytime," said Mel. "Are you still moving into my spare bedroom after the holidays?"

She bit her lip. "Um, of course. Nothing's changed."

"You're always welcome. But if you have crazy sex with your ex and can't bear to leave that behind, I'd approve of that, too. You deserve some good sex this holiday season."

Selena rolled her eyes. "Aww, thanks, Mel. Wishing you the same."

She hung up and blew out a breath. Crazy holiday sex with Jace? She was definitely not going to distract herself with that idea right now. She finished making the mac and cheese and the cocktail sausages, poured herself a cup of coffee, and brought it into her office. Her studio was across the hall from her bedroom suite, in what would have been a guest room if Darren had had his way. It was east-facing with beautiful morning light, or as much light as December mornings in Upstate New York came with. Flat, wide art tables lined the perimeter with a half-dozen projects in various stages of production.

She sat down at her sketching desk and took a sip of her coffee. Talking to Mel was always a boost and a good reminder—she didn't have to take this run-in with Jace so seriously. Seeing him again could be fun...and sexy as hell if they didn't get stuck on the past.

But for now, instead of trying to block out these thoughts, maybe she should make a card out of them. Hmm, something like *I know I broke your heart but I still wanted to sex you up today*? Who knows? It might be a common enough sentiment to warrant a card.

CHAPTER FIVE

 Jace stood outside his brother's front door, his hands in his pockets. He was late, a sin worse than absence in his mother's mind, but he still hadn't brought himself to knock. The half-frozen rain had stopped not long after he'd left Selena's car at the garage. After he found her overnight bag and a few packages in her back seat. After he had debated whether to drive back to her place and give them to her, knowing he'd want to kiss her again.

 So he'd resisted, but his mind was still filled with her. Selena. Long brown hair and those dark eyes. Her hair still smelled so good, and he could remember the shape of her face with his eyes closed. Jace had moved on years ago, so why were all these details coming back? Most vivid were the scenes from their Friday nights by the beach. How many times had they sat in his car, talking or laughing or just quiet, but holding each other, always touching. More often than not, she'd fall sleep against his chest, but he'd stay awake, fighting his own drowsiness so they didn't miss her curfew. Even one slip-up would've meant the end of their Friday nights together, and no amount of sleep was worth that.

Jace touched his mouth, where her soft lips had pressed against his less than an hour ago. Seeing Selena today had been just like falling down that rabbit hole again, into hot, erotic heaven. But there were differences that had niggled at him since he found her at the side of the road, and on the ride back to the garage, he was still trying to put his finger on what they were. Kissing was the same, maybe even better. And she looked just as lovely as she always did. It was something else. At eighteen, he could feel her happiness, the fresh excitement of *becoming*. Now, nine years later, that energy and excitement hadn't shone so brightly, and he wasn't quite sure what had taken its place.

His memories of Selena were so old and well-worn that they had dulled at the edges, but today, they sharpened back into focus, reminders of all the reasons he still wanted to hold her and all the reasons why he never should let his mind wander in that direction again.

Jace massaged his temples. He'd have hours alone in his bed to worry about that. Tonight was for Andrew and Mary Louise. Which meant he absolutely couldn't mention Selena under any circumstances. No one wanted reminders of his lowest point nine years ago, including him.

He closed his eyes one more time, tasting the whisper of Selena's lips on his once more, and then shut all those memories down. At least he had nine years of practice with that, too. He let out a sigh, straighten up and knocked on his brother's door. It opened almost immediately, and his mother stood in the doorway, frowning at him.

"You're late."

"I'm sorry."

She smelled of her favorite flowery perfume, the kind she put on for special occasions. Tonight was important for her, and he was late.

He leaned forward and kissed her on the cheek, ignoring the trickle of guilt that ran through him. "I had a tow call. And it's not a good night to be stuck out on the road."

"You could have let one of those big companies take care of it." His mother knew very well that the "big companies" didn't come this far north very often, and even if they did, they charged an outrageous fee. It had only been a year since Jace's father stroke, not nearly long enough for her to forget any of this. Jace didn't have to explain to her that staying in business meant serving a niche. And if they didn't offer more personal service, they'd never compete with the bigger companies.

But that guilt still seeping in. None of those were the real reason he had taken so long. The real reason was Selena, she who must not be named. So he let his mother's comment go, the way he had let so many comments go since his father's stroke. This last year hadn't been easy for her, and he knew family meals were the highlights of her week.

His mother was still hovering in the doorway, so he kissed her cheek again and slipped by her. "Are Andrew and Mary Louise somewhere in here, too?"

"Andrew and your father are in the kitchen. Mary Louise, your sister and I are in the basement, working on some wedding details."

Easy choice. "I'll go in find Dad and Andrew."

Jace started through the hallway toward the kitchen. The house was only a few years old, his brother's newest masterpiece in a portfolio of beautiful homes along the Lake Ontario coast. He had designed it with his own love of cooking in mind, so in addition to the top-of-the-line appliances, the entire back wall of the kitchen was lined with windows that faced the lake. This was what going to college did for his brother. Jace had tried hard not to think too much about what it would have done for him.

He found his brother in a dress shirt with his sleeves rolled up, standing on one side of the bar counter over a roasted turkey. Jace smiled as he read Andrew's apron: *One of us is right. The other is you.* Probably a gift from Mary Louise, proof that she knew what she was getting into by marrying him.

His father was on the other side of the counter, sitting in an armchair his brother must have brought in for him. Jace's father had a hard time getting around on his own, even after a year of rehab on his left side, much to his ongoing frustration. He still worked half days in the garage. Though office work had always been the bane of his existence when he was in charge, Jace was pretty sure it was often the best part of his day now. Nothing like a twist of fate to give you a new perspective.

Jace walked over to his father and gave him a squeeze on the shoulder, then grabbed a beer from Andrew's fridge.

"Lookin' good," he said, giving the perfectly browned turkey another glance.

"I experimented with baking soda under the skin," said Andrew. "Figured this was a good crowd to try my new ideas on. Minus Mom, of course."

Their dad gave a snort of laughter. It was no secret where Andrew's my-way's-the-right-way attitude came from.

"Just say you got the idea from some British Royal cookbook," said Jace, taking a swig of his beer.

"You know she's already read all of them," said his dad. True.

His father's speech was slower now, and in a large family with a long history of talking over each other, it had taken some adjustment. The smaller the group, the better, and, frankly, it was a hell of a lot easier to make room for his father in the conversation without his mother. Talking for him was her way of worrying about him, so Jace was trying hard to be understanding, but sometimes…

He propped himself in the corner of the kitchen and took a swig of his beer. "Let me guess. Drake can't make it tonight."

Andrew smirked. "Emergency at work."

"What a surprise," Jace said dryly.

Their older brother had moved to New York City after college and had been working seven-day work weeks since. Not that Jace was one to judge, especially considering the fact that he had just come from the garage, but at least he made it.

"So," his father started, "W-what kind of a car was your tow?"

Jace stiffened. He didn't want to get into the particulars of this car. Or its owner. But his father had taught Jace everything he knew about cars, and now that he could no longer work on them himself, he lived vicariously through Jace. This was their point of bonding...usually. So he gave his father the bare minimum.

"Mercedes, newer model."

His father narrowed his eyes, and for a minute Jace was sure that he knew exactly whose car it was. But then his father waved his hand dismissively. "Whoever owns that car has taken shitty care of it if it's already breaking down."

Jace let out the breath he had been holding. His father didn't know what kind of car Selena had. Of course not. Jace was the only one who had been watching her from an uneasy distance since she came back.

"Definitely neglected." He hoped his father hadn't heard the gruffness in his voice. It hadn't just been the car that was neglected. After the way Selena kissed him in her hallway, he had all sorts of ideas about what else had been neglected and what he could do about it. Though he was trying like hell not to have those thoughts right now.

"What color was it?" His brother's voice startled him and his dad jerked his head around to Andrew. Andrew put his hands up. "Just trying to get in on the male bonding that goes on in this family."

Like hell. Andrew had made it clear that he had zero interest in cars. Jace knew exactly what Andrew was doing, and he swallowed back a few choice words for his brother.

His father had turned back to Jace, waiting for the answer, so Jace shrugged, like the question meant nothing. "Red."

The lack of reaction on his face told Jace that his father still had no idea whose car it was. But Andrew knew. And there was no way in hell he was going to let his older brother open this can of worms for the family—not until Jace knew what the hell he was going to do about it.

"You can come on down to the shop and check out the color, Andrew," he said dryly. "See if you have any expert advice."

His father smirked at that. Usually his brother would have bristled at this comment, which would have led to a few rounds of insults, but Andrew wasn't easily distracted. He was staring at Jace, and with one eyebrow raised, he manage to convey all the same doubts that had been circling in Jace's mind since he answered Selena's call. Could anything good come out of seeing her again? Was heartbreak worse the second time around? What the *hell* was Jace thinking?

Their silent stalemate fizzled out as voices floated from the basement, growing louder. Footsteps thumped up the stairs, and Lizzy appeared first. She tipped her chin at Jace, smiling.

"You're late."

"So I've been told," he said, trying his best to wipe all traces of emotion from his face. Lizzy's smile faltered a little, so he turned away to give Mary Louise a kiss on the cheek. Talk was filling the kitchen, the way it always did in the Wilkinson family, but Andrew was still standing by the turkey, uncharacteristically quiet. Jace circled the counter and stood next to his brother under the guise of helping.

"Not a word, Andrew," he muttered under his breath. "Especially not around Mom. I mean it."

His brother shook his head slowly. "This is not a good idea, Jace. You've managed to avoid her since she came back into town. There's no reason why things can't continue that way. I know you've both moved on, but—"

"She called for a tow, for Christ sake. Was I supposed to leave her by the side of the road, just because things ended badly however many years ago?"

"You know exactly how long it's been since you've seen her."

It was true, so Jace said nothing, just stare down his brother, willing him to leave the subject alone. "It was just a fucking tow, Andrew."

"Maybe. But you and I both know how easily you could get caught up in her again."

It hurt to hear those words spoken aloud, even if they were accurate. All the giddiness from kissing Selena had dissolved. He already knew how their story ended. In the end, she left.

These thoughts were exactly why the subject of Selena was not up for discussion.

"This conversation is over," grumbled Jace. "And don't fucking mention this to anyone."

Andrew had the nerve to chuckle. "I definitely won't ruin Mom and Dad's day with this bit of information. But beyond that, I'm not promising anything."

CHAPTER SIX

The next evening, Jace parked his pick-up in front of Selena's house and turned off the engine. The rain pounded on the windshield, echoing inside the cab. Andrew was right. He knew Andrew was right. But he'd spent the entire drive coming up with reasons why he still should check in with her in the middle of a storm. Because she was alone with no car, and the storm was getting worse. Because Andrew and Mary Louise had sent him home with too much food, and it shouldn't go to waste. Because he'd forgotten to get Selena's phone number for the car repairs. Because she had left three packages in the back seat of her car, including one from her parents, all the way from Mexico, which she probably wanted to open.

But all of these reasons were excuses. The truth was he just wanted to see her again, now that he had had a little time to digest their first meeting. No expectations, just deliver the packages and the food and head home. Though getting everything to her doorstep in good condition would be a challenge.

The neighborhood still looked empty, though a couple houses glowed with soft lights. Next door to Selena's place, a car was parked in the driveway. A Hummer. Who the hell drove one of those things? The kind of guy that owned a beach house in this rich-ass neighborhood, apparently.

Jace peeked up at Selena's house again. The chains of tiny white lights glowed through the house. And then he saw her in one of the windows, hunched over something. He was too far away to see much more than just her hair and the shape of her face, but it didn't matter. His heart jumped in his chest, and he closed his eyes.

Her teenage bedroom had faced the street, right on the porch that stretched across the front of her house, and there were nights when he'd drive by and see her, studying at her desk. Sneaking in was out of the question, and she'd never sneak out, despite the fact that she was only a few feet from the ground. But he'd park out of sight and tap on her window, and they'd talk in whispers for hours. And kiss, too.

Nine years had passed, and if he was in a reasonable mood, he could understand her choice. Her parents had left their home country behind and moved to the United States. They'd figured out how to pay for new degrees when employers wouldn't take their original ones, and they'd passed up promotions that would have moved the family or split them apart. For most of Selena's life, her parents had given up any semblance of comfort to make sure their only daughter had opportunities they hadn't. And it weighed on every single choice Selena made. Including her choice of men.

But even if he could sympathize with her dilemma, he was not—and never would be—a consolation prize. Why the hell was he still thinking about this? Andrew was definitely right. It was too easy to get caught up in her again. Maybe he should just go home.

Jace rested his fingers on the ignition and glanced once more at the window where she sat. Sleet streamed down his truck, and he had to lean across the cab to get a better view. This time, she was looking out into the darkness, right at his truck.

Damn.

It was too late to drive off, not if he didn't want to look like a stalker. Besides, it was better this way. She was out here alone, and if he had driven off, he would have spent the night thinking about her, wondering if she was okay. Now, he would probably be spending the night thinking about her in much different ways.

The image was there before he could stop it. His body over hers, her fingers digging into his arms as he—

Shit. He swiped a hand over his face and shook his head. Enough. He'd deliver the packages and the food and get his ass home.

Jace grabbed the bag of Tupperware dishes and stacked the boxes on top of each other. He took a deep breath and opened the truck's door. A gust of rain hit him in the face, but he pushed forward, balancing the teetering load under his chin as the door slammed shut. He dodged the puddles that were pooling at the base of her driveway and headed up to the house. The awning above her porch did nothing to stop the icy water from pelting at his back. This delivery idea was looking worse by the minute.

He knocked, and Selena's face appeared in the frosted glass. She opened the door and stared at him.

"Jace?"

"Yeah, me," he said roughly. "I just wanted to drop off—"

"Get in here," she said, tugging on his arm. "You're letting the rain in."

He stepped inside, and she pushed the door shut and locked it. They stood in the muted quiet of the little entryway, the storm pounding at the door. Close enough to touch. Selena blinked up at him, her eyebrows raised in question.

"I, um, brought the packages you left in your car," he finally said.

She blinked.

"Oh, right," she said quickly, reaching for them. Her warm hands brushed against his, and she looked away. "Thanks."

His gaze drifted down her body slowly, taking in the oversized Christmas sweater, her red-and-white striped leggings, and a pair of red socks. He fought a smile. She definitely wasn't expecting company tonight. His eyes drifted back up a bit. The candy cane pattern hugged the curves of her legs… Damn, he was ogling her. Jace's gaze snapped back to her face.

"Oh, right. The outfit," she said, smiling. "It's…"

"Colorful?"

She chuckled. "Very diplomatic of you."

"I like it."

The beauty of Selena's smile was in her eyes. When she really smiled, they sparkled and laughed and tempted him to be the one to make her happy, again and again. But that wasn't how their story went. What he felt now was just the echo of old memories and the undercurrent of lust that was deeply woven between them.

Time to leave.

He took one last drink of that smile, but this time he saw something more in her eyes. Desire. Like he wasn't the only one who had spent the day thinking about that kiss in her doorway. And he just couldn't make himself go. Instead, Jace lifted his hand to her face and traced a path down her cheek with his fingers. Her smile faded, and her cheeks flushed.

"Want some company for a while?" he asked softly.

She bit her lip, and her brow wrinkled. Her gaze traveled down his body, taking him in. He was dripping on her front hall carpet, and the bag of leftovers still dangled from his hand. Then, a hint of a smile quirked at the corners of her mouth.

"Company would be nice," she said. "You should warm up, and I still have your blanket."

Jace nodded, his heart thumping in his chest. He let out a quiet sigh of relief as he bent down to unlace his boots. They were just spending a little time together, nothing serious. He stepped out of them and slipped off his coat, hanging it by the door. The desire, the spark of connection after all these years wasn't just his overactive imagination. Maybe they could suspend the past for just a few hours.

Jace followed Selena up the stairs to the open living room and kitchen. The place was impressive, with its high ceilings and exposed beams, even more so considering that he had heard it was a second home. The room was filled with expensive-looking furniture, curtains, blankets, and a bunch of other crap someone else probably would appreciate. A little potted fir tree sat in the corner, sparsely decorated. A string of white lights lit it up, and more of them glowed around the big stone fireplace and the large windows.

Jace walked over to the kitchen's island and set down the bag of food.

"The bathroom down the hall has a shower if you want to warm up," she said and held out his blanket. "Just set your wet clothes outside the door and I'll throw them in the dryer. You get to be naked under a blanket this time."

He chuckled and took it from her.

"What's in the bag?" she asked.

"Leftovers from the engagement dinner last night," he said. "Turkey, mashed potatoes, two kinds of pie. A step up from cocktail sausages."

"I already ate," she said quickly, turning away from the food.

He surveyed the kitchen. An empty bowl, a glass, and a few cocktail sausages left in a skillet. She couldn't be *that* full. But the food was from his family, one of their many complications, and her message was loud and clear: *Let's keep this simple.*

His eighteen-year-old self might have been hurt, but he had nothing to lose with this woman tonight. Jace gave her a little smile, shrugged and started down the hall.

"Suit yourself. I'll go get naked."

CHAPTER SEVEN

Bad idea. Jace was in her house, and she had just pointed him toward the shower and told him to strip. Now she couldn't get the thought of his naked body out of her mind. The water running down all those muscles…

At least that's what she remembered about him: smooth, hard muscles across his chest and arms and stomach. There was a time in her life when Jace was hers, and she had been too torn about whether they had a future together to fully appreciate it. If she had a chance to explore again, just for a little bit, she'd—

Stop. Selena froze that thought before it went any further. If she did any exploring of Jace's muscles again, it wouldn't—couldn't—be tied to the past.

She walked toward the bathroom and grabbed the clothes Jace had dropped on the hallway floor. All of them. His pants were soaked through, but his shirt was only wet around the collar, where the rain had seeped down the opening in his raincoat. Um, she wasn't going to stare at his boxers, wondering what he'd look like taking them off. She buried them in the pile and gathered it in her arms.

The scent of Jace hit her hard. The shirt smelled like him, and the memories flooded back faster than she could stop them. It felt good, so she let her mind travel down that road just a little more. Sitting on his lap in his car, the one place they could be alone.

She and Jace had been careful, so careful. How many times had they parked by the beach and eased the front seats back? She'd learned to wear skirts on Friday nights senior year, so she wasn't squirming out of jeans in the passenger seat of his Corvette. Positions, firsts, and so much fun. She'd given him his first blowjob there. It had lasted thirty seconds max, and he narrated the experience with all sorts of swearing and groaning that had her both giggling and turned on. And then he had gone down on her.

A rush of pleasure ran through her. Shit. She was standing in her hallway fantasizing about her teenage sex life. Who had her best sex at eighteen? Hopefully, not her.

Selena gave a quiet snort of laughter and headed downstairs. She threw the clothes into the dryer, then returned to the kitchen. The island countertop was loaded with Jace's wet delivery. She peeked into the bag of food, and the smell of pecan pie flooded her senses.

She inhaled the sweet, buttery scent. If she had chosen to return Jace's calls, to come back the summer after her freshman year instead of taking an internship in Boston, would she have spent today eating pie and celebrating Andrew's engagement, too? Selena sighed. Maybe. But she would have probably dropped out of college. He'd wanted her to stay so badly, and when they were together, she had wanted it, too. That was the problem. If she had dropped out of college, she never would have forgiven Jace—or herself. How many times had she gone over the choices she made?

Selena resealed the lid and blinked her eyes a few times until the burning subsided. It was too much. Time to shut off the past and focus on the present. She pushed the bag aside and unstacked the three, damp packages from the back seat of her car.

The one from her parents was the smallest. What would they send her? Something in silver, something to remind her of the little town they'd finally returned to, with help from her and Darren. Darren had been generous early on in their relationship; that much she could say about him.

The door to the bathroom opened, and Selena looked up just as Jace emerged from the steam. With only a towel wrapped around his waist. Oh, God he was gorgeous. Jace had filled out in the best way possible, his shoulders wider, his arms bigger. There was a spray of hair across his chest, and the trail down to his towel was a little thicker.

Her gaze darted up to his face as her cheeks heated up. No gawking at her high school boyfriend allowed. His too-long hair hung over his forehead, uncombed, and his lips quirked up in a smile.

"The blanket is a little scratchy," he said. "Got anything else?"

He sounded almost apologetic, as if he knew what being nearly naked with her might do for both of them. Maybe he was just as wary about dragging that up as she was.

She shrugged and smiled. "I have some flowery beach dresses that might fit."

Selena stole another glance at his bare torso as she passed him. She could have married this man. She bit her lip and forced her gaze on her bedroom door.

Jace followed her in, dressed in only a towel, the water dripping off his hair. She didn't even need to turn around to know that. The image of him walking out of the bathroom was imprinted firmly in her mind. She opened her dresser drawers, sifting through shirts and leggings.

"It's all on the small side," she mumbled.

He bent over her shoulder, peering down into the piles of clothing. What had caught his attention? Then she saw it. Buried deep in the stack was Jace's old high school football sweatshirt. She had kept it all these years.

He was right behind her, near enough to feel his breath in her hair. She remembered this, the way it felt to be so close to him, the way she could feel his mood without looking. The electric pull between them grew stronger, and her heart pounded in her chest.

Selena pulled out the sweatshirt and handed it to him over her shoulder. "I should have given this back a long time ago."

He didn't move. His breaths stopped. After a long pause, he took the sweatshirt, his hand brushing over hers. Then he stepped away, breaking the current between them.

She turned back to the drawer and searched until she found a t-shirt his size. She had originally bought it as a gag gift for Darren, though he hadn't thought it was funny. Yet another sign of a bad match. But it fit right into her collection, so she'd kept it. She slipped it out of the pile and handed it to Jace, and he held it up.

"*Abs are nice but doughnuts are better*," he read aloud, chuckling. "Nice."

She closed the drawer and opened another, searching until she found a pair of Darren's old green cut-off sweatpants he hadn't bothered to take with him, *Winner* printed on the rear. In her sock drawer, she found a fluffy pair of bright red socks. The more ridiculous the outfit, the better to keep the mood between them fun. Which was the key to enjoying this dose of alone time with Jace…and letting it go, unscathed.

Smiling, she handed them over to him, making sure her gaze didn't drift down from his face to his bare chest. "If I'm dressed like this, you get a colorful outfit, too."

"'Winner'?"

"Make your own conclusions."

His smile was way too cocky for his state of undress. Right next to her bed. Time to get out of there.

So she left him alone in her bedroom and returned to the kitchen island. God, he still had the same effect on her as he did all those years ago. Before she could brace herself for another round of Jace, he wandered into the kitchen. No more bare chest. Still hot, but the quirky outfit took the effect down a notch. Much better. He planted his hands on the island counter and studied her packages.

"From your parents," he said, nodding to the little brown-wrapped box at the center.

She frowned. It was a little too personal, a little too intimate to discuss her parents with him. It was no secret how hard they'd pushed her to break up with Jace, to move away and set her sights on college instead. And the second package was from Darren's sister, another topic she didn't want to get into.

Selena pushed those two boxes aside and focused on the third one. The return address had no name, just a P.O. Box in Delilah's Cove, Oregon. She bent down for a side view, but there were no other clues.

"It's not gonna open itself," said Jace, his voice laced with humor.

She wrinkled her nose. "I don't know who it's from. But Delilah's Cove sounds familiar."

"Are you sure you don't know? Or are you just waiting for me to leave so you can open those sex toys you ordered?" He picked up the box and shook it a little. "Hmm. If it's a vibrator, it's heavy. Do you get a discount if you order in bulk?"

"What would I do with a bulk load of vibrators?"

Jace put up his hands in surrender, snickering. "I'm not judging."

Selena rolled her eyes. "Give it to me."

She tore through the tape and opened the unmarked brown box. Inside was a round tin with a Christmas wreath on the lid. Four travel-size bottles of booze were packed in next to it. On top was a blank white card. She glanced up at Jace, and he raised his eyebrows.

"Come on," he said. "You're killing me."

She waggled her eyebrows and turned over the card in slow motion. Jace groaned.

"*Enjoy the magic of Christmas and prepare to fall in love*," she read. "The note is unsigned. Just those words and a web address from the USA Times."

She set down the card and lifted the tin out of the box. Then she picked up one of the travel-size bottles with a laugh. "An anonymous gift of Wild Turkey? What the hell kind of Secret Santa is this?"

"A damn good one," he said. "Open the tin."

She had forgotten how impatient he could get.

She looked up at him innocently and batted her eyelashes.

"This tin?" she asked, pointing into the box at the remaining item. She gave him a wide-eyed look, stalling. "You want me to open it?"

"Open it, *Lee*."

She stilled. *Lee*. The nickname he used to use. He was standing close, dressed in his old football sweatshirt, calling her Lee. Her heart surged and her chest tightened, as she fought the warm flood of memories. Selena bit her lip and opened the lid, and the smell of whiskey filled the room.

Inside the tin was a fruitcake. An alcohol-laden one, clearly.

Selena burst into laughter.

"A fruitcake?" she managed between snorts. "Who sends a fruitcake?"

She looked up at Jace, and he was smiling, his eyebrows raised.

"What?"

"You got one of them."

"What are you talking about?"

"You got one of the Delilah's Cove fruitcakes." He bent over it and took a whiff. "You didn't hear about this?"

She shook her head.

He picked up the card and pointed at the web address. "I didn't know anything about it until the USA Times ran an article on it early last month. It's all very secretive. No one knows who makes them or who will get them."

Selena took the card from him and studied it. *The magic of Christmas? Fall in love?* She wrinkled her nose and studied it. "I'm just supposed to ignore the fact that it's crazy to eat it an unidentified fruitcake that shows up in my mailbox?"

Jace shrugged. "Someone baked a cake, added Wild Turkey, bought four more little bottles to throw in the box, wrote a card and paid to send it to you. If it's a hoax, it's pretty damn elaborate."

Selena furrowed her brow. "I still think it's a little nutty."

Jace laughed. "Are you making bad fruitcake jokes?"

"Evidently," she groaned.

They both stared at the fruitcake on top of the island. The rain whipped and pounded on the windows, cutting through the silence of the kitchen.

"Go for it, Selena. You know you want to open up the Wild Turkey."

He clapped his hands together, like they were breaking a football huddle, and once again, her chest tightened. It was Jace, standing in her kitchen, talking her into something, just the way he used to.

She had told herself so many times that it hadn't been love between them, just hormones and sex with a side of teenage drama. Hell, she had even told Darren that when they bought this house, and most of her had believed it. But as Jace smiled at her, his face lit with excitement and pure joy, she couldn't lie to herself anymore. There was so much more to them than hormones and sex, things she hadn't let herself remember. There was more to their story than the very end. They'd had the closeness from years of knowing each other, watching each other struggle. She *had* been in love with this man all those years ago.

What would happen if they added a little alcohol into the mix tonight? Looking at him over this crazy fruitcake, she wanted him to smile at her the way he had moments ago. Could she put aside all the reasons this might not be a good idea, just to see what would happen if they spent a few more hours together? Since Jace showed up, the sting of the revelations about Darren's new life had faded. Nothing wrong with enjoying herself, enjoying *them* again…right?

She looked back up at Jace. His smile had faded.

"Just an idea," he said, looking away.

"This has some serious whiskey in it," she said. "If we do it, you'll have to keep me company for a while longer before you can drive again."

He met her eyes, and his brow wrinkled a little.

"You don't have to," she added quickly. "We can just—"

"I want to." He cut her off, and for a moment, he looked at her the way he used to. Hungry. Like he wanted so much more than just to keep her company.

Right now, she wanted that, too.

Selena bit her lip. "Let's do it."

The corners of Jace's mouth curved up again, and he grabbed a little bottle of Wild Turkey. "Hot damn, we're trying the legendary fruitcake."

She chuckled as she lifted the heavy cake out of the tin and placed it on her countertop. It was Bundt-shaped and brown with nuts and raisins, as well as bright red and green bits of something sticking out of it. Not chocolate cake-level appetizing, but it could be decent. Maybe, with enough Wild Turkey.

"I've never actually seen a fruitcake in person," she said.

"Me neither."

"Are there any instructions? Should I read the USA Times article first?"

For a minute, Jace looked almost anxious. If it had been nine years ago, she would have asked him what was wrong. Instead, she tried to read his reaction, something she used to be good at. But the look vanished too quickly, and in its place, he gave her an easy smile. "Sure, read it. See what you think."

Selena grabbed her phone out of her purse and typed in the web address, then scrolled through the article.

"You've got to be kidding me," she said, setting down her phone. "People really believe in magic?"

"Naah," he said. "Probably just a publicity

stunt."

But as he spoke, he tilted his head and stared down at the fruitcake, as if he was still thinking through her question. The rain against her windows echoed in the warm kitchen as the silence between them grew. What if, against all odds, there really was something special about this anonymous package?

Prepare to fall in love.

Selena took a deep breath and handed him the bottle, then pulled out a basting brush from the cooking drawer. "You pour, I'll brush."

He unscrewed the top and a fresh wave of Wild Turkey filled the air between them. With a little laugh, he drizzled it on, and the alcohol disappeared into the cake. She brushed the baster over the trail of Wild Turkey Jace had left, with little effect.

"I think we did that wrong."

He shrugged, still grinning.

Selena walked over to the cupboard and grabbed two plates. She set them on the island and nudged Jace aside to open the silverware drawer he was blocking.

He moved, but after she grabbed the forks and a large cake knife, he came up just behind her, his warm body so close, then settled against the counter. Her heart was doing crazy things in her chest, but she kept her eyes trained on the fruitcake.

The knife sliced through the cake easily, and Selena slid a piece onto each plate. Jace grabbed one. When she passed him a fork, his fingers lingered on hers as he took it. Heat rushed to her cheeks and down her body, spreading everywhere.

She cut off a bite and lifted it with her fork, finally meeting his gaze.

"To unexpected gifts," she whispered.

Emotion flashed in his eyes, something she couldn't quite read. He raised his bite. "To unexpected twists of fate."

CHAPTER EIGHT

What the hell were they doing? From the moment Selena had unwrapped the fruitcake with the USA Times web address on the card, Jace had known exactly what was sitting on her counter. The magic fucking fruitcake. The one that was supposed to make people fall in love.

Ever since the beginning of December, the whole town had been talking about the ridiculous article. He usually ignored that kind of thing, but Andrew had had a lot to say about love these days. His brother was always looking for a reason to talk smack about how Jace thought he was too good for the women who flirted with him at the garage. About how one day some woman was going to bring him to his knees. So while he was supposed to go over the details of a classic Mercedes 1955 Gullwing Coupe, his brother had pulled the article up on his phone and read the highlights aloud. An anonymous sender, a cryptic note, and a fruitcake that had people falling in love. Bullshit. It must be the Wild Turkey talking.

"Maybe whoever is behind these fruitcakes will take pity on you, bro," Andrew had said, slapping Jace on the back.

"It would take a hell of a lot of magic to make me eat fruitcake. Forget the falling in love part," Jace had said to his brother.

But there he was, in the middle of Selena's kitchen, eating a piece of the goddamn fruitcake. What had compelled him to talk her into tasting it? It had taken him years to get over her, so it couldn't be that he wanted to go through that again. And he definitely didn't believe in magic. But when he put the note together with the article Andrew had read to him, all that he could think about was this: What if Selena ate it when the pizza dude came for a delivery? Or if the neighbor with the Hummer came to check on her, and they ended up in bed?

Hell, no.

He didn't believe in this magic bullshit, not even a little bit. Still, he wasn't willing to take the risk. Magic or self-fulfilling prophesy, if there was any chance that Selena would fall in love with someone, he wasn't letting another man step in. The last time, she ended up with that tool Darren. This time, he wasn't taking any chances.

Jace swallowed down the bite of cake and raised his eyebrows. Surprisingly good. He took another bite and glanced over at Selena. She was staring down at her near-empty plate, her brow furrowed. Like something had just occurred to her, something that had surprised her. Slowly, he took another bite, his eyes fixed on her.

"This fruitcake is actually tasty," she mumbled, a bit of wonder in her voice.

Jace's mouth was full, so he grunted in agreement. No declarations of love yet. The magic was probably just gossip, something that Sacred Harbor already had more than its fair share of. He wasn't disappointed. He had just tasted the damn cake to make sure. Nothing wrong with that.

Selena frowned. "What do you think is in it?"

Jace snorted. "A cup or two of Wild Turkey." He took the last bite and nodded over to the empty skillet on the stove. "Anything would taste good after cocktail sausages."

"Hey, I like that stuff," she said, giving him a little shove.

"This is better." He loaded up a bite on his fork and glided it around like an airplane flying toward her. "Open up."

Selena rolled her eyes.

"Come on," he said with mock seriousness. "Where's your sense of adventure?"

She sighed, and he headed the fork toward her again. But as she opened her mouth, he swooped it away and ate the bite himself. Selena huffed in exasperation.

"You're such a child, Jace."

He lowered the fork and turned to move closer to her, their bodies almost touching.

"Not even close," he whispered.

She licked her lips. Goddamn, this woman did something to him. He loaded up the fork one more time and slowly brought it to her lips.

"I don't know if I trust you this time," she said.

Was she talking about the airplane game or something more? Maybe it didn't matter. The last couple of days had already taken enough crazy turns for him to start second guessing it now. Her call in to the garage. The bomb she'd dropped about her divorce and full-time residence just outside Sacred Harbor. The anonymous fruitcake package. He probably should have hightailed it back to his house long ago. But he hadn't. He was here, facing his sexy ex-girlfriend, and the Wild Turkey was starting to take effect on him. Which meant it was surely getting to her, too. He did a little loop with the bite of cake loaded up on the fork.

"You can trust me, Selena," he said. "You know me."

The corners of her mouth turned up. "That's the problem. I know you well enough to know this is probably a bad idea."

But she didn't move away. Her lashes fluttered closed, and she parted her lips. Damn, the temptation was overwhelming. And it was so hard to remember why he was resisting anymore. Time to stop resisting. Instead of feeding her another bite of fruitcake, he leaned over and brushed his lips against hers.

A sharp inhale. A moan so soft he almost missed it. Then she leaned forward and kissed him back. Her lips lingered against his, their breaths mingling.

Yes. Yes. He had thought about this so many times since he dropped her off. The taste of her lips. Her scent. Her body shifting closer. Now it was happening again. Selena was kissing him. Tomorrow, he'd be kicking himself for getting tangled up with her, for letting the tiny spark of hope come alive inside, hope beyond reason that the rumors of magic were true. But right now, that didn't matter. Nothing else mattered when the relief of kissing her was running through his body.

Or maybe it wasn't relief. Maybe it was something else.

She opened her eyes and looked up at him. Lines creased her forehead, and she bit her lip. But before she could say anything that would take away from that kiss, somehow make it less, he lifted the fork again.

"Is this what you're looking for?"

Selena laughed, and the wrinkle on her brow disappeared. He fed her the cake, and she let out a little sigh of pleasure. His heart thudded in his chest as he watched her. What the hell was he getting himself into?

"You win," she said, swallowing the bite. "This is so much better than cocktail sausages."

The rain splattered in gusts across the tall windows, obscuring the sand and the water. Not a good night to be driving, even sober. But it was getting harder and harder to imagine a scenario that wouldn't bring him to his knees before he walked out her door. He was so aware of every move she made, every nervous fidget of her hand, every time she bit her lip. Was she thinking about where this night would go, too?

Selena set down her fork. "I think we should…"

She paused. What was coming next? All sorts of endings to that sentence raced through his head.

I think we should take off our clothes.

I think we should see if sex between us is as good as it used to be.

.

CHAPTER NINE

"I think we should do a shot of Wild Turkey."

Selena bit back her smile as Jace let out a bark of laughter.

"That's not where I thought you were going with that sentence," he said.

Selena lifted her eyebrows in challenge. "Is that a yes or a no?"

She headed for the glassware cabinet before he caught her blush. He was just as perceptive as always. That wasn't what she had meant to ask. She was about to say they should give that kiss one more try. Knowing full well that it wouldn't stop at a kiss. Instead she chickened out and opted for reinforcements of the alcoholic variety. Not too much, just enough to keep her mind off the past, to keep her focus on the way it felt to be with Jace right now.

"A shot of Wild Turkey, and then I want a tour of your house," he said.

She nodded and brought over two low

tumblers, and Jace twisted off the cap of another little bottle. He poured a finger's worth of whiskey in each. Raising his glass, he waggled his eyebrows at her. "To holiday pleasures."

"Are you coming on to me, Jace?"

He shrugged, and the corners of his mouth quirked up. "You want me to?"

Her cheeks flushed as she flashed to the kind of holiday pleasures she could have with Jace. "I still haven't decided."

Jace threw back the whiskey and set the glass onto the island counter. "Your turn."

Selena took a sip of hers, and Jace shook his head.

"Nope. The whole thing. Your idea, by the way."

She tipped her head back and let the liquid burn a trail down her throat, swallowing the last bit with a cough. Jace raised his hand for a high-five, his eyes filled with delight, and she slapped it.

"I'm glad I'm here to witness this." He took her glass and set it aside. His hand slipped around her waist. "Now let's take a tour of your house."

Her heart thumped hard in her chest, and the whiskey was making her a little giddy. Or maybe it wasn't the whiskey. Jace's hand stayed on her hip as they wandered into the living room. It was the same way he'd always used to touch her, just a reminder that he was there. But as they passed her couch, his arm snagged around her waist, and he pulled her down on the plush pillows, onto his lap. She laughed and wriggled, but he held on tight, so Selena relaxed against him. She took a deep breath, catching his warm, outdoor scent, and sighed.

"I like this couch," he said, and his deep chuckle sent warm bolts of pleasure through her. He patted the pillows, testing them. "Big enough to sleep on. Or do other things."

She smiled and shrugged. He shifted so he was facing her, his dark eyes intense.

"You never tried?"

She wrinkled her nose. "Nope."

"Hmm," he said softly.

If she had lived here with Jace, they would have given the couch a try long ago. As well as most of the other furniture. Was he imagining alternate histories for them right now, too? His eyes sparkled with pleasure. She rested a hand on his bicep, and he let out something between a sigh and a groan. God, it felt so good to be close to him again.

Then his smile faded. He raised a hand to her cheek, the way he had when he kissed her the day before in her doorway, and for a moment she thought he was going to kiss her again. But he didn't. There was plenty of heat in his gaze, but there was something more, too. Creases formed in his brow.

"You're not married anymore," he whispered.

She shook her head slowly.

"But you split up not that long ago."

It wasn't a question. What did he want to

know? Was he wondering whether she was still hung up on Darren? This wasn't her favorite topic.

"You sure you want to talk about it?" she asked.

Jace chuckled. "Not sure how to answer that. But, yes, I want to know."

Behind his laugh, Selena could hear his hesitation. It was hard for him to ask. What could she tell him? That there was a time she thought she loved Darren? That he had admired her drive, at least at first? After the divorce, she had even wondered if she had been attracted to Darren because of just how different he was from Jace. Because she didn't want to be reminded of him. Because she didn't want to miss him so badly.

But now she was sitting on Jace's lap. His arm was wrapped around her, and his hand slowly stroked up and down her side. It felt so good to lean into his warmth, with the rain softly pelting the glass. Trying to explain any of the whys of her relationship with Darren might hurt Jace, even if her relationship with Darren was long over. The closeness between her and Jace was still fragile.

Selena looked away, squinting out into the darkness, weighing her words. "I talked to his new girlfriend when I was in Boston a couple days ago. I dropped by to pick up those packages you brought."

"Was that hard?" he asked, his voice quiet.

She nodded. "We fought for years about his traveling, and he said he had no control over it. That it was the nature of his job, that I'd known that from the beginning." She swallowed back the lump in her throat and continued. "But apparently, it wasn't. Because he got a new job, no travel, just for Lizzie's kids. And Darren didn't even want kids."

She looked over at Jace. His eyes were dark, his gaze probing.

"I'm glad Darren wasn't there when I stopped by," she added. "I probably would have said a bunch of things I'd regret."

That earned her a hint of a smile. "I bet you would."

"Yeah. Probably double my humiliation level."

His eyes widened. "Humiliation? Why?"

She shrugged. "That's what I felt on that day my car broke down. Definitely. But it's better now."

His arms tightened around her, and she closed her eyes, sinking into the comfort Jace was offering. Comfort for the mistakes of her marriage to the man she'd chosen over Jace. Was he putting aside his own feelings for her?

Her heart gave a jolt. The Jace she'd known at eighteen wouldn't have comforted her like this. He couldn't have. Or maybe her eighteen-year-old self had been too caught up in her own struggles to hear it. But this moment was new, different. They were different. Maybe it was time to clean the slate between them.

Selena bit her lip. "I made some hard choices,

Jace. I thought they were the right ones at the time, and now I can't change them. I just want to make the best of where I am now."

Her comment was about more than just her marriage. It wasn't an apology for leaving for college—she wasn't sorry for that—but she could have handled it differently. If spending time with Jace again felt this good, this right, she needed to move beyond the regrets of her past.

He pulled her closer and kissed her neck, sending rays of heat through her body. The soft lights, Jace's warm body, and her heart pounding away in her ears all came together in a quiet happiness she hadn't felt in a long time.

"I made mistakes, too, Selena. Mistakes I wish I could take back," he said, his voice husky. "It was wrong of me to pressure you to stay in Sacred Harbor."

She stilled in his arms. After all those months of trying to make him see why she needed to leave for college, all those months of accusations and fighting, this was the last thing she thought she'd hear from him. She turned to meet his gaze. Longing and regret simmered with the heat in his eyes. And maybe she even saw loneliness.

"I don't regret asking you to marry me," he said, his voice a low rasp. "But I do regret tying it all together, making you choose between me and college. I just couldn't imagine four years away from you."

"I couldn't imagine it, either," she whispered.

"That's why I left without saying goodbye. I was afraid I'd change my mind."

She had tried so hard not to think about him when she'd left, losing herself in the newness of college, of living in Boston. Blocking out all the hurt, trying so hard to turn off the physical ache of being away from him. Up until recently, she had lived that other life. It had been a good one in many ways, but there were things that she had promised herself would be more satisfying if she just hung on a little longer. Things like love and contentment.

Nine years had passed, and here she was, lying with Jace's arms around her, his slow breaths in her ear. Was the happiness running through her just an echo of their past, or could they make it into something new?

Too much to think about right now.

He shifted so his long legs stretched across the couch, and she settled between them. His breaths slowed, and she closed her eyes, the way she used to on his parents' couch. She might have nodded off because, when she opened her eyes, the buzz of the Wild Turkey shot was gone. But she was still surrounded by a wall of warm, hard muscles. It felt good, really good. A scary kind of good.

"Jace?"

"Yeah?" His voice, rumbling and full of sleep, sent a new rush of desire through her.

"If we're doing this...whatever we're doing together, we need to be friends, too."

"Weren't we friends back in high school?"

She laughed. "We certainly didn't spend our Friday nights the way friends do."

He didn't answer right away, but she was sure he remembered. His mouth brushed over the top of her head, and he pulled her tighter. "You don't want to do that anymore?"

"I do." Lord, did she ever. "Though maybe not in the front seat of your car."

He chuckled softly, his chest moving under her. Then he sighed. "I see your point. And not just the one about the car."

The past was gone, and it would hurt, digging into it, looking back to the way things were. But now that she'd opened this new door, invited Jace in, laughed with him, slept in his arms again, she wasn't ready to leave him in the past. They had to look forward. But it was so easy to let her guard down with him, and whatever this was between them felt vulnerable. *She* felt vulnerable. So Selena took her time, searching for the right words.

"Falling asleep with you feels good," she said softly. "Really good. And it's really tempting to just fall back into this, you and me together. But I think we both know all the reasons we need to be careful, too."

She could feel his nod against her.

"We should spend time just talking," she continued. "Go to coffee or something."

"Coffee?"

"Friends do that. Not that I have any friends around here as examples, so you'll have to take my word for it."

"Hmm…" He stroked her hair, then slid his hand down her arm. He found her hand and wove his fingers with hers. "Okay, *friend*. Let's meet for coffee."

CHAPTER TEN

Selena walked along the shoulder of the road, sidestepping mounds of melting snow. Late during the night, the rain had turned to beautiful, white flakes, but it wasn't sticking, making for a slushy mess. She hoped it wasn't an omen for what was to come because she was already having second thoughts about this plan. Buying coffee for five dollars at a café was the most ridiculous way to spend her money right now, when finances were tight. Plus, she was on deadline, which meant she shouldn't waste precious morning hours, the hours she was most productive, on a social call. And yet, she was braving the cold to meet Jace at the Harbor Café. Like friends would.

Maybe friends was a bit of a stretch, since she was dying to do things with him that had nothing to do with friendship. But, luckily, reason had won over hormones the other night. The connection was strong between them, which meant this new-found intimacy could so easily hurt both of them. Maybe the hurt couldn't be avoided. She was still planning to leave Sacred Harbor after the holidays, of course. But when

Jace appeared on her doorstep, wet and bearing gifts, her heart had stuttered in her chest.

Was Jace the reason why she had dragged her feet this fall instead of putting the house on the market? Just a few days ago, she would have rejected that idea completely. But could she trust her reasoning around him when she had worked so hard to leave him behind? Maybe, somewhere inside, she had stayed because she needed to know if those long-buried feelings were gone for good.

And now that they'd seen each other, talked, even fallen asleep on her couch together, she couldn't stop thinking about him. Or maybe this was just the effects of that "magical" fruitcake. In which case it should be wearing off soon, if her knowledge of magic was accurate. That knowledge came entirely from fiction, of course. Selena rolled her eyes. This whole situation was crazy.

She turned the corner of the last block and headed toward the lake, her wool scarf high on her neck, shielding her from the sharp gusts of wind. The weathered wooden building was right next to a harbor, with a deck overlooking the lake and the shoreline, so the place got a lot of business during the summer. Hopefully, right now it was empty. Hopefully, no one would recognize them. That had been a selling point when she planned this coffee date—that and the fact that Selena hadn't been outside in two days. She pulled her scarf up further, over her mouth as she neared the water. The temperature here wasn't so much colder than it was back in Boston, at least not so far this year, but there was a hell of a lot more space between everything, giving the wind a strong advantage. Plus, after nine years away, she had forgotten how to dress for this kind of cold, apparently.

Selena opened the door to the café, and a rush of warm air blew over her face and found its way under her scarf. Her shoulders unclenched a little as she took a step in. The place was bright and decorated for the holidays with garlands and strings of lights. Small candles were lit on each of the wooden tables, and the whole place smelled like cinnamon rolls. Maybe it was worth a five dollar cup of coffee.

But then she saw the stares. The place was far from empty, and everyone there was looking at her. No one seemed familiar, at least not at first glance. Maybe this was a bad idea.

Then she saw Jace, standing in line with his back to her, his unruly hair and broad shoulders still familiar. He had taken off his jacket, showing off how unfairly fit he still was. Did he play sports these days? There were so many things she didn't know about him anymore.

Then he turned around, and his face lit up when he saw her. All her worries about this meeting dissolved, and for one moment, she wanted everything she used to have with him, all over again. And she was in so much trouble if that's how she was thinking. The past was gone.

"Hello, *friend*," he said, his smile full of humor. Then he gave her the kind of kiss that was *soooo* not in friend territory. His lips opened against hers, lingering, sending a new wave of that same desire that had bombarded her since he kissed her on her doorstep.

She pulled back a little and looked at him. He wasn't smiling anymore, but his eyes were warm and welcoming. So familiar.

"Here we are, having a nice friendly coffee," he whispered. "No bedrooms involved."

Not yet, at least. But, oh, how she wanted to kiss him again…and more. She wasn't sure how long she could resist, but she owed it to herself to try, at least for a little bit.

"I just think we should talk a little," she said, inching away, "and not about the past. Just catch up, be around each other. See if we even still like each other."

"I'm pretty sure I still like you," he said with a smirk.

"Being attracted to someone is not the same as liking them."

He opened his mouth like he was going to argue, but then he shook his head. "Okay. Let's do this."

She ordered a coffee, and Jace tried to pay but Selena insisted they each buy their own. Like friends. He raised an eyebrow but didn't comment. They made their way to the corner table, and Selena kept her head down as they found their seats. The table was small, and their legs tangled together in a very un-friend-like way, but she didn't pull back. The truth was that she was happy to sit like that with him. It felt like *them* in the best way possible. She drank her coffee in silence, just watching him, and his gaze was fixed on her, too. With anyone else this kind of staring would be uncomfortable, but with him it didn't seem to matter.

But she came here to talk, to slow this down a little, to try to be friends, so she broke the silence. She asked him about the garage, his family, his house, and he asked about her life in Boston, though they both skirted around the topic of Darren. And the more she sat in that quiet corner of the café, together with Jace again, the more the happiness simmered inside.

After a pause, Jace opened his mouth, hesitated, then spoke. "Do you think your parents knew how serious we were back in high school?"

"Maybe," she said. "Maybe they were willing to look the other way as long as I didn't get pregnant went to college."

"They got their wish."

"Still, here we are."

"Yes, here we are," he echoed. He looked out the window. "What would they say if they saw us here together? They thought I was a bad influence."

"You were," she said, smiling. "Do I need to mention Friday nights again?"

Jace laughed. "That's fair."

Selena considered his question. "Honestly, I think they'd be fine. My mom used to give me updates about you when they still lived in Sacred Harbor. I think a part of her wanted us to find a way back to each other."

His eyes blazed bright as he looked across the table at her. "She can get that wish. If that's what you want."

She swallowed back the lump in her throat. But they needed more than just feelings. Before she let the idea of *them* into her head, they needed to consider what path they could take together.

"What are your dreams these days, Jace?"

He blinked in surprise and then the corners of his mouth hitched up. "Not the first question I'd ask a *friend*, but I'll go with it."

His smile faded, and he looked out the window, quiet for a while. "This last year has been so much about my dad's stroke. He was really depressed, and running the garage has been a big part of his recovery but…" He paused and ran his hand through his hair. "But with the garage all on my shoulders, his happiness so wrapped up in it, I'm not sure how long I can hold that up. I'm going to try for him, but my dream is that my life could be a little more than that."

She nodded. Back in high school, when his dad had leaned on him for relief, Jace didn't seem to mind. But now, when the business rested on his shoulders alone, she could see why it would be different. She and Jace were still so young. Did he, too, wonder what this long stretch of life in front of them was supposed to be about?

"Your turn, Lee," he said, his voice gentle. "What are your dreams?"

"I've always wanted to make my parents proud. It sounds strange to be an adult and still thinking about that, but it's true. My parents gave up a lot for me. And I think my divorce was just as hard on them as it was on me."

Jace frowned. "I doubt that."

Maybe he was right, but her parents had struggled to understand her divorce. Why would she leave a life that was everything they'd wanted to give her?

"I don't mind hard times, and I'm okay with struggling," she said after a while, "but I want to know that it's for something worthwhile in the end."

Jace was watching her the whole time she spoke, she felt he was really listening.

"There is a lot of disappointment in life," he said softly.

She nodded. "But I can accept that if there's joy in it too."

He was quiet for a while, his brow furrowed. His shoulders rose and fell, heavy, and it felt like he was debating something. Finally, he sighed. "Was there joy in your life with Darren?"

*

He really didn't want to know the answer, but he couldn't stop himself. At least he hadn't asked any of the other questions on his mind. *Did you love him with all of yourself? Did he give you all the things I couldn't give you?* So Jace settled with the question about joy, though that one was hard in a different way. The selfish part of him didn't want her to find happiness with someone else, and yet, knowing Selena wasn't happy for years was painful, too.

It took a while for her to answer, and when she did, she didn't meet his gaze. "I thought there was joy at first, but after a while I realized that the feeling wasn't happiness itself. It was excitement about what I *thought* was coming. Not about the way things were but about how they might be. And then, after years of waiting, I understood that what I thought we were working for—it wasn't ever going to come."

Her words felt heavy, and they drove home the bone-deep wish he had struggled with since he lay on her couch with his arms around her. She had had some tough years, and he wanted to be the one to change that. He wanted another chance, a chance to find a new kind of happiness together with her.

He reached across the table and covered her hand with his. She didn't pull away, just looked down at his hand, studying it.

"How long are you staying in Sacred Harbor?"

"I was planning to put the house on the market months ago," she said. His jaw tightened, but he stayed quiet. "My friend Melanie has a spare bedroom where I can stay while I look for a place in Boston."

"You have a job waiting for you there?"

She shook her head. "I could probably get one or continue to freelance, like I'm doing now."

He swallowed. "And that's what you want to do? Move back to Boston?"

"I don't know," she whispered.

She lifted her gaze, and they studied each other the way they had when they sat down. The reality was that his chances to see her would probably end soon. But he was older this time, if not wiser then at least a bit more patient. He had pressured her all those years ago, and he wouldn't make the same mistake again. *Give her time.*

"Just think about it, Lee," he whispered, and he left it at that.

Selena turned her hand over and fit it into his. Her fingers were still cold from her walk outside, and he stroked his thumb over her skin, warming it. After a while, she looked up at him, smiling, her eyes twinkling with mischief.

"Do you want to come over tomorrow and finish your tour of my house?"

"Very much."

She laughed softly, almost to herself. "This is not even close to a friend conversation."

Jace shook his head. "You know we could never just be friends."

CHAPTER ELEVEN

Jace's question about staying in Sacred Harbor hovered over Selena's thoughts like an incoming cloud bank, the kind that said, *Things are about to get serious*. So, of course, she was trying to ignore it. She needed to turn in the preliminary sketches for her Easter project so she could focus on her personal and, as of yet, unpaid projects.

She had managed to focus for a few hours, but the closer evening came, the more the idea of staying played through her mind. What would it be like to stay in Sacred Harbor for real? Since leaving Boston four months ago, she had deliberately avoided making her life here feel permanent. It was supposed to be recovery from the divorce after the final terms were settled. Just a little time to regroup and then she'd return to Boston.

But what was waiting for her there? Melanie, her one friend that was truly hers, not Darren's. Mel was definitely a reason to go back, and she'd welcome Selena into her apartment for as long as she needed. But her friend traveled a fair amount on research trips, and Selena was pretty sure she wouldn't live there forever. Melanie wasn't on speaking terms with her poet father, but Selena got the feeling that if her father ever reached out, Melanie would be on the next plane to Stockholm.

The truth: There was no reason she *had* to move back to Boston. She could work from Sacred Harbor, like she had for the last few months, and she could still stay at Mel's place when she had in-person meetings.

It wasn't that Boston was calling her. The question was whether staying in Sacred Harbor would be a step back, into the past, or a step forward, into a future she wanted. Oh, how easy it would be to go back to life with Jace at the center. At the café she could feel the connection between them growing stronger. The more time she spent with him, the more she wanted. It had taken all her strength to leave him behind nine years ago, and it wouldn't be any easier the second time around. Maybe worse, now that she knew that, even after nine years, the connection between them sparked back to life so easily.

So staying in Sacred Harbor wasn't just a question of giving their relationship another chance for a few weeks, just to see how things went. Staying was bigger than that. Either she wanted a second chance with him, a real go at this as two adults, with eyes wide open, or she needed to walk away from him forever.

Tonight Jace was coming over for a tour of the house, a thinly veiled euphemism for what she had fantasized about every night since he had picked her up in the tow truck. Maybe what they felt was mostly nostalgia, and the reality wouldn't be nearly as satisfying. Or maybe it would be more. But she needed to choose to either give this a try for real or set them both free. And he had to choose, too.

Selena only understood that she had been pacing when Jace's knock startled her out of her path. "Coming."

She made a quick stop at the hallway mirror and smoothed her t-shirt over the roundness of her stomach. The tour of the house was likely to end in the bedroom, quite possibly with their clothes off. She had gained weight since high school, and there was no way he had missed it. But this was her *now*, not the memory of her, so maybe it was better this way. Different. No illusions. Selena swept her hair over one shoulder and headed for the front door.

And there he was, standing at her doorstep. The snow was falling in big, wet flakes, covering her porch in a blanket of white. He stood in the middle of this winter wonderland, almost like a dream. She had had dreams like this long ago, dreams where somehow Jace showed up on her front door, and somehow they were together again, like they were in high school.

But this wasn't that dream. He looked tired. She could see it now in the creases on his forehead and the heaviness in his eyes. But he also looked happy to see her, as if she was the relief he had been waiting for all day.

Selena grabbed his hand and tugged him inside, closing the door behind him. Then she unzipped his jacket and slipped her hands inside it, finding her way to his warmth.

"No food or packages this time?" she asked, smiling up at him.

Jace chuckled. "You want a package? I have one, just for you, if that's what you're looking for."

She rolled her eyes and groaned. "Teenage humor."

His grin faded, and his eyes grew heavy with desire. "We're not in high school anymore. Not at all."

His voice was low, and he took a step toward her. She smiled and stepped back. He took another step and another, until her back was against the wall. Then he bent his head down and kissed her. No, this definitely wasn't high school. Back then, their kisses had been sloppy and eager, but they were older now, more experienced, and he knew how to take this devastatingly slow. Jace kissed like he was speaking to her. Each soft stroke of his tongue over hers said *stay*. Each graze of his teeth over her lips said *I'll make it good for you*. Each caress of his hand through her hair said *I promise*. It was the kiss to define all future kisses, and he was giving it to her as she teetered on the precipice between leave or stay. It was hard to think, so she just kissed him back without hesitation, getting lost in this man who made her feel like no one else did.

Too soon, far too soon, his hand left in her hair, and he pulled back.

"Hi," he whispered, his lips brushing against hers.

She was breathless, dizzy from the kiss. "Thanks for coming."

"Anytime." He said it with an intensity that took her breath away. But then he stepped back, his warm body gone as he shed his winter clothes and boots.

"So…" Selena searched for what she was going to say before that kiss. "Do you want some fruitcake?"

"Exactly what I was thinking."

She let out a snort of laughter. "Sure it was."

He followed her up to the kitchen, and she could feel his eyes on her, taking her in.

The fruitcake was still on the counter, a healthy piece of it missing from the other night. She cut two more slices and laid them on plates, passing one to him. Her hand slowed as she caught sight of the card from the package, right where she'd left it.

Prepare to fall in love.

Was that what they were doing? She looked up at him, and they both stilled. Was he wondering the same thing? Selena looked away, not ready to answer that question, not yet. Jace took the plates to the counter and sat down on a bar stool, and she slid onto the stool next to his. He rested his thigh against hers as he took his first bite, and her heart skittered. They ate and talked about their days, and it was so easy, so natural, the way it had been at the café. But there was something more, too. This time, the bedroom was near, and she felt that knowledge zip between them, an electric charge that made each brush of her leg against his more vivid.

So she set her fork down on her empty plate, leaned over and pressed her lips against his.

"You still want that tour of the house?" she asked.

Do you still want to take this further?

He rested his forearms on his thighs and hung his head for a moment, shaking it slowly. When he looked back up at her, he was smiling. "Oh, Selena. You know that I'm up for just about anything with you."

He turned to face her, and she slid off her stool into the space between his legs. She rested her hands on his thighs. "Ready?"

He laughed and nodded, and she headed for the hallway with Jace close behind.

"What's downstairs?" he asked, pointing to the staircase that led down from the front door.

"The laundry room and two more bedrooms," she said. For the kids she and Darren never had.

Jace nodded, then poked his head into a bathroom and a closet.

"What's that room?" he asked, pointing to the

door across from her bedroom.

"My studio."

She opened the door and turned on the light. Jace walked in, scanning the room. He had knocked on the door while she was working, so everything was still a mess. Photos and sketches littered one desk, while another held watercolors in various stages, drying. Still another was reserved for larger acrylic paintings. The desk in front of the window was for polishing up a finished project. It had the best natural light, so she used it for getting a good look at a piece. Or for rethinking her career.

"Nice," he said. "Looks like you've got a lot going on."

"I contract for two different greeting card companies, and each of those projects are at different stages. I split them by desk to keep them straight."

He grinned. "I saw you through the window when I pulled up."

"I was hoping for a little more inspiration today," she said, "This hasn't been my most upbeat year."

"Mmm," he murmured, then laughed. "You mean no one wants a 'fuck you very much for the divorce fallout' card?"

Selena gave a dry laugh. "You should have seen my Valentine's Day portfolio this year. It was awful."

He nodded slowly. "What's the solution?"

"Put on my cheerful pants." She gave him an

exaggerated, toothy grin, and he chuckled.

"Hmm…is that working?"

She shrugged. "Sometimes."

"Can I see some of the results?"

Selena bit her lip. If this was the first night, she probably would have said no. But this was Jace. He wouldn't care if next season's Christmas cards were a little… inappropriate.

She walked over to her desk, and he followed her close behind, resting a hand on her hip. She turned around to face him, her body blocking his view. His fingers stroked her waist, under her t-shirt. His smile was slow and easy, and his gaze wandered down to her lips. He was waiting for her, as if there was nothing in the world he'd rather do.

"I'm experimenting with new markets this next year, and it might mean printing the cards myself. My first sketches were too gloomy, so I went for, um," She paused, searching for the right word. "Raunchy. Just so you know."

Jace's smile grew. "Now I'm even more curious."

She opened a drawer in her filing cabinets and pulled out a folder, setting it on the desk next to her. Jace's gaze lingered on her for an extra beat, and then he opened it, flipping through the preliminary prints of the cards. He let out a snort of laughter.

"*Wishing you a well-hung Christmas?*" he read, holding up one of the cards.

She had painted a close-up of a suggestive-looking ornament on a tree, right on the border of inappropriate. Without the words, the subject matter might not be obvious, but with them... well, it was clear.

"Is that what's inspiring you this winter? A well-hung Christmas?" His voice grew deeper, as his laughter faded. His eyes were bright and warm. She wasn't sure what was happening between them, but she was willing to go along with it as long as she'd be lying naked with him soon.

She tilted her head. "You offering?"

He smiled. "I guess I am."

CHAPTER TWELVE

It's just sex. It's just sex.

Maybe if she chanted that sentence enough times, the message would sink in. Because now that Selena had let the idea in her head, she couldn't stop thinking about what it would be like to be with Jace again. Really be with him.

Hot? Almost definitely.

But intimate, too. His body brushing against hers, his deep voice, his hand on her hip, stroking gently—each sensual detail was a trigger, leading her back to the way it had been all those years ago. There were times when she felt so raw, so bare. Could they have some sexy fun together, or would it leave them both vulnerable? She was about to find out.

He was so close now, his familiar scent surrounding her and his eyes, hungry.

Take it slowly. Nothing serious.

So Selena crossed her arms and lied. "Well-hung? I don't really remember…"

Jace tipped his head back and laughed,

shaking his head. "You sure you don't remember, Lee?" When he met her eyes again, his expression had a hint of seriousness. "Because I remember everything about you. Everything."

"Remind me," she whispered.

"First I want to see your t-shirt."

"What?" She wrinkled her brow at his non-sequitur.

"You had a drawer full of t-shirts with all sorts of sayings on them. I want to see what you have on now."

"It's not raunchy, if that's what you're wondering."

"Are you stalling?"

"Nope." Well, maybe she was. In an attempt to make this evening about who they were today, she had decided against dressing up. Instead, she grabbed an old standby t-shirt that said, *Cute but CRAZY*, the Z backwards, with a bat hanging from the Z, teeth bared in a wicked smile. But now that they were in the bedroom, the shirt felt more childish than fun. Still, this was Jace. Selena found the hem of her sweatshirt and pulled it off.

"Cute but crazy?" he read, staring at her chest. "I like that in a woman."

She rolled her eyes. "Sure."

Jace tilted his head to the side, as if he were considering his next words carefully.

"You came with some drama, Selena," he said. "Especially those last months when we were together. But I liked your kind of crazy."

"And what kind is that?"

"The kind that's fun and sexy and so goddamn hard to forget."

She took a steadying breath. How many times did she have to tell herself that this was just sex? Her stupid heart still hadn't gotten the message. *Thump, thump, thump*, it pounded in her ears as the spark between them brightened.

Enough talking. Enough thinking. It was time to get to the good stuff.

"Are we done with the tour?" she asked.

He smiled. "I could make a really classy comment about the kind of tour I'm interested in next."

Selena waggled her eyebrows at him. "Would you like a private tour, Jace?"

"I want to do my own exploring."

His laugh was so sexy, and it was just for her. She had forgotten how much they used to laugh together. That deep ring of his voice awoke another flood of memories. Saturday nights at Ruth's Pizza Place. Movies on his parents' couch, his little sister squished onto the couch with them. She had buried these memories, hidden them from herself, but the more time she spent with Jace, the more they came back.

He stepped closer and tugged gently at the bottom of her shirt. "Can I take it off?"

She nodded and lifted her arms, and he

brought the shirt over her head. His expression grew more serious as he traced the edges of her bra with the pads of his fingers. She looked down at her body, heavier, nine years older.

"I'm not as…perky as I used to be," she said, her cheeks heating up.

His brow furrowed a little. "Selena, I promise you that judging your body is the last thing I'm concerned with."

She swallowed. "It's hard to miss."

"You want to know what's going through my mind right now?" he asked, his fingers running over her stomach.

She nodded.

"I'm thinking, goddamn, did I really spend nine years without you?" he whispered.

Selena closed her eyes and swallowed hard. The more he touched her, the more he whispered in her ear with that husky voice, the more serious this felt. And she didn't want it to stop.

"Can you take off your shirt?" she asked.

He smiled and tugged it over his head. Selena stilled as her pulse kicked up. When he walked out of the bathroom shirtless, she had wanted to take time to stare. Now, she did it. Oh, Lord, this man was gorgeous. He was built, but in a different way than she remembered, leaner, more muscular, more…man. How unfair it was that he had gotten more beautiful and she had gotten rounder. But he seemed just as captivated by her as she was by him. In fact, maybe he was waiting for a response.

"Not bad," she said, though her words stuck in her throat.

Jace chuckled. "Aww, thanks."

"I just don't want it to go to your head."

"Who me?" He flexed his muscles in a couple of exaggerated poses, then cracked a smile.

Selena did her best to look unimpressed, but she was pretty sure she was failing. "You still play any sports?"

He shook his head. "Rarely. One injury and the garage is in trouble. We can't afford it."

"I didn't think about that," she said softly.

But he didn't look bothered by it, at least not right now.

"Your turn to strip," he said, crossing his arms.

She reached around and unfastened her bra, letting it drop to the floor. His gaze was intense, his eyes half-lidded with desire, and he took a step toward her, but she shook her head.

"You're next."

He slipped off his socks and jeans…and then his boxers. No hesitation. He was hard and naked and ready and so, so close. When her gaze finally wandered back to his face, his smile bordered on smug.

"Your turn again."

She slipped off the last of her own clothes, and they stood facing each other, naked in every way.

His hands glided over her shoulders, down her arms. He traced her collarbone, her breasts, her stomach. It took a moment to remember that she could touch him, too, so she did. The muscles of his arms, the tufts of hair on his chest, the ridges of his abs, and lower.

Jace drew in a sharp breath, followed by a little laugh. "I want you too much to play around. It's been so long."

She smiled and took a step back to the bed, trying to ease the weight of his comment. *It's been so long.* They had both moved on after she left, and yet he said these words like he had been waiting for her. Maybe some part of her had been searching for a way back to him, too.

Jace followed her toward the bed, mirroring her first step, then her second, his big, warm body pressed against hers. She scooted onto the mattress and lay back, propping herself on her elbows, studying more of the changes. Jace had lost all traces of boyishness. His shoulders were broader, his muscles more defined. He had also lost some of that easy smile he had worn as a teenager, though it seemed to be coming back as the night progressed.

His chest rose and fell as he gazed down at her, his eyes hooded. The way he looked at her hadn't changed at all. Like there was nothing else that mattered except her.

But it wasn't like that anymore. Did she want it to be? If she let her mind wander down that long-forbidden path for just this moment, what would she find?

"Something else on your mind?" Jace's voice broke into her thoughts.

She motioned him closer. "I'll whisper it in your ear."

He chuckled and climbed over her, resting on his elbows, the delicious weight of his body on top of hers. He kissed her lips, her neck and her lips again.

"What are you thinking about, Lee?"

"Us," she whispered. "The way it used to be with us."

Some of the truth, not nearly all of it.

Jace's deep chuckle rumbled in her ear. "Good. So good."

The tightness inside eased a little, so she tried to put more of her thoughts into words. "You think it might be just as good this time?"

"Maybe. Or maybe it'll be better." He kissed her again and flexed his hips, his erection pressing against her.

She lifted her head to brush her lips against his. "I'm on birth control. Just thought you might want to know."

"I've never been with anyone without a condom. Ever. But I brought one. In the back pocket of my jeans."

"Because you knew you'd get lucky tonight?"

Jace shook his head, but he didn't answer right away. Selena got the feeling he was debating how much to reveal. Then he licked his lips and spoke. "Because I'd never want to miss this chance if it came up."

She lay on her back and brought her hands to his face, stroking his cheeks, running her fingers over the stubble of his jaw. "So you think we might be good together the second time around?"

His gaze moved over her slowly, hot and intense. "I hope so."

Hope. That was the right word for this moment. Looking up into his eyes, she let herself hope. Want. Maybe even *need* the things they could give each other.

So they kissed and kissed and kissed some more. She parted her legs, and he settled between them. He reached down, teasing her, getting her even more worked up. His erection pressed urgently against her thigh, and she wiggled closer.

"You want this?" His voice was short and a little strained.

"Yes. *Yes.*"

He lowered his head for a kiss, first soft, then hungrier as he entered her. *Oh, God*, there was nothing that came close to this magical mix of bliss and relief. Finally, *finally*, she and Jace were together again. He shifted over her, memories mixing with sensations as they fit themselves together.

Selena closed her eyes, adjusting, remembering. Jace was inside her, covering her with his big, hard body, the familiar scent of him everywhere. She didn't resist the flood of happiness that filled her. *At last*. Jace shook as he held her, waiting for her.

"I'm ready," she whispered. "Please."

He rested on his elbows, pulling out and then gliding back in. Pleasure raced through her, every stroke spreading white-hot bursts of desire. She met each of his thrusts, pulling him against her, trying to get closer. It was as if all those years apart were just to lead them to this moment, when they came together again. His muscles moved against hers, and he wrapped his hands around her shoulders, holding her in place as he thrust. His eyes were dark and serious, and he didn't look away.

"Goddamn, Selena," he bit out. "There's no one like you."

She moaned and met each of his thrusts with her hips, faster, harder. The connection between them was so good, so strong, and he whispered words of pleasure, over and over, telling her how much he needed her. His expression tightened and his breaths were fast and harsh. He was close, but she knew he'd wait for her. He always would. Selena blinked back her tears as her body burst into flames.

CHAPTER THIRTEEN

Jace's body was spent, but he held Selena tightly, breathing in her scent. He wasn't ready to let her go. Her head rested on his chest, and her legs tangled with his. Their bodies still fit together so perfectly.

He could feel the moment starting to slip away, and he searched for something to say, something to convince her to hold onto this new connection, to explore it.

"I meant what I said," he whispered into her hair. "There's no one like you."

Selena's body shook with quiet laughter. "We can do that again, if that's what you're asking."

"That's not what I'm talking about."

She stilled in his arms. "You don't have to explain."

He shook his head. He had to get these next moments right. What could he say to convince her to start over with him?

"Jace?"

Her voice was soft, hesitant. Selena's hand

drifted over his shoulder and down his arm, and her eyes were serious.

Jace flipped his hand over and laced his fingers with hers. "Please don't just disappear. Give us a chance."

Now he had said it, and he braced himself for whatever came next.

"I've been thinking about it. A lot." Her eyes were dewy, and it was doing crazy things to him.

"I'm not going to push you this time," he said, keeping his voice even. "But I can't be casual with you."

If this ended again, Jace wasn't sure if his heart would survive it, but he didn't want to let her go. He had already tried a life without her.

"I don't think I can be casual either." She squeezed his hand. "We probably should have known that from the start."

"Maybe we should talk about it. About us." Her voice was so soft, barely there, but his heart jumped in his chest. Was she ready for a new beginning, or was this the end?

He shifted to his side so he could see her expression. He didn't want to miss anything.

Selena drew in a long breath. "I know this isn't the past, but I don't want us to make the same mistakes again."

"Me neither." It felt too soon to bring up their break-up, but he wasn't going to say no to her. Maybe she needed this conversation to move on. "Where do we start?"

She propped her chin on her hand and smiled a little, but her eyes were full of questions. "Going away to college and leaving you was the hardest thing I've ever done. I was so in love with you. But in all those months of trying to coax me to stay in Sacred Harbor, you never once offered to come to Boston. You could have, you know."

Her lips shook as she spoke, and he wrinkled his brow. She had wanted him to come with her, yet she had never said it. If she had asked, would he have said yes, leaving his family and the garage behind? Maybe, but it would have been a painful choice.

"And it's not like you were at home waiting for me," she continued. "Mary Jo Whitney made sure I knew about the blow job she gave you on Valentine's Day that year. How she understood why I had been with you all through high school."

Jace closed his eyes. "It wasn't—"

"We weren't together, Jace," she said quickly. "I'm just saying that when I called you that spring, things had changed."

He shook his head. "Not for me."

"Then why didn't you say so?" Her voice was tight.

Jace furrowed his brow. "I don't know. Because you wouldn't take the ring. Because my dad needed me at the garage." He closed his eyes. "And maybe because I needed to grow up a little more."

She let go of his hand and moved closer,

resting her cheek on his shoulder. "I needed to grow up, too. Eighteen is too young to get married."

"Maybe."

It felt so good to be close to her again, her body touching his. Nine years ago, all he had wanted was for Selena to come back, for everything to be the way it had been. His life was here, his family, his garage, everything that meant something to him. But he had been so scared of losing her, scared that she'd leave him behind for a guy with more money, more education. And in the end, she had.

Now, he was trying to wrap his head around how it felt to be her back then. She had wanted college, and she wasn't ready for marriage, but she still wanted him. At eighteen, all he could hear was the rejection. Even though he would have said he loved her ambition and drive, he had tried to pressure her to stay back. All because he didn't want to lose her. A heaviness was settling in his chest.

"I'm so sorry, too, Selena," he said. "I shouldn't have made you choose. If I could take it back, I would."

She nodded. "We're not eighteen anymore. Maybe we can both do better this time around."

Jace slipped his other hand to her waist, stroking up and down. "Whatever happens next with us, I promise I'll do better."

She turned to him and held his face in her hands. Slowly, she guided his mouth to hers. He kissed her softly.

She pulled back a little, blinking up at him. "Do you think this is just the magical fruitcake talking?"

It took a minute to remember what she was talking about.

"You're kidding, right?" He frowned a little. "I can't imagine a scenario where I don't want you."

Selena took a deep breath, and her eyes softened as she studied him. "But there's something magical about us meeting again, isn't there? My car breaking down, you picking me up, me leaving my packages for you to bring back. Though you forgot my suitcase in the trunk."

"It's outside in my truck. You distracted me." Jace laughed as he gazed down at her, smiling. "Maybe it's not the fruitcake. Maybe we're making our own magic."

"Are we giving this a try for real, Jace?"

Her eyes were bright with the same hope that had been brewing inside him since they sat across from each other in the café.

"Yes. For real," he said, sliding his hand over her collarbone and down her chest. He cupped her breast, and she sighed with pleasure. "Tomorrow is Saturday, which means we can spend the whole day in bed. We can make up for all those years apart. And then you can come with me to Sunday brunch at my parents' place."

Selena's mouth dropped open, so Jace kissed her again before she had a chance to protest.

CHAPTER FOURTEEN

Selena glanced over at Jace, standing next to her on the snow-covered front porch of his parents' house. Fresh flakes of snow dusted his hair, and his breaths puffed out in faint clouds. He was rubbing his hands together absently, staring at the door, but he hadn't made any move to open it. Was he having second thoughts? She certainly was.

She slipped her hand into his back pocket and tugged him closer. "Are we really ready for this?"

"Sure we are…in a trial-by-fire kind of way," he said with a little laugh. Then he reached for her hand and laced his fingers with hers. "Seriously, we can handle my family."

"I'll be fine," she said, more to herself than to him. "I used to love coming here." Most of the time, at least. In the end, it was harder. Seeing his mother for the first time in nine years? That part probably wouldn't be as fun.

Jace gestured to the gift bag with cards sticking out of it. "You didn't have to bring a gift."

"Just chocolate," she said. And a couple other things…

"Plus, Drake's here for the weekend. My mother will spend a good portion of the evening convincing my brother to visit more often, so she can see all four of her kids at the table." Jace flashed her an innocent smile. "I'm one of the good sons, remember?"

It was a valid point, but…"And I'm the ex-girlfriend that broke the good son's heart."

"That's the past." He turned to rest a hand on her face, stroking her cheek. Snowflakes fell through the air between them, landing on his eyelashes, his coat, everywhere. His gaze wandered to her lips, and he bent down for a soft, warm kiss. "This is about us today. And whatever happens tonight, I owe you anything you want for a day."

"Anything I want for a day," she repeated. "That does have its appeal. You'll be washing dishes, doing the laundry, shoveling snow…"

Before she could continue, Jace's mouth was on hers again for another kiss, this one hungrier. "I was hoping your demands would be more along the lines of me going down on you, sex in the shower, a dirty—"

The front door of his parents' house creaked open, and Selena froze. *Classy way to start the evening.* She took a deep breath and turned around. But it wasn't his mother standing in the doorway. It was Lizzie, and she was so far from the girl she had been the last time Selena had seen her.

"You two planning on making out on the doorstep all evening, or are you coming in?"

Selena just stared at the woman in front of her. When she had left for college, Lizzie had been an adorable eleven-year-old kid. Now, she was gorgeous and tall, taller than Selena by inches. She looked like Jace. It shouldn't have caught her off guard, but a lump rose in the back of her throat. So much time had passed.

Selena probably would have stood there, gaping for a lot longer if Jace hadn't tugged her hand.

"Welcome back," said Lizzie softly. For a moment, his sister look vulnerable, as if she, too, had worried about this dinner all day.

So Selena set aside her own worries, took a few steps into the warmth of the house, and wrapped her arms around Lizzie. She sighed and hugged her back. It felt so good to see her again, and Selena struggled to focus on that part, not on all the years she had missed.

She pulled back a little. "Look at you. It's been a long time."

"A lot happens in nine years."

"Don't I know it."

The entranceway was silent for a moment as they watched each other. Then Lizzie dipped her head and turned down the hallway. "We're all in the kitchen. Drake just got here a bit ago."

Selena took off her coat and scarf, handing

them to Jace, trying to process that this young woman walking away was the same girl she had left. Nine years ago, she was still a kid, so happy to watch movies with Jace and her or play board games or do any of the other things families did together— families whose parents weren't so exhausted from a day of work that they collapsed in the evenings.

Though Jace was the biggest heartbreak that came with leaving Sacred Harbor, he wasn't the only one. In that first year after she left, Selena had ached to see Lizzie, but she had known better than to contact her. Even on the chance the call might have been welcomed, Jace's mother would have put an end to it, and there was a chance Lizzie would have dealt with the brunt of her mother's bitterness. So Selena had left that alone. Maybe a second chance with Jace meant she and Lizzie could be close again, this time as adults.

Jace found her hand again and waggled his eyebrows at her. "No turning back now."

"I'm ready." Hopefully.

Jace's parents' house was so familiar it almost hurt to look around. Each photo on the wall, each embroidered throw pillow unlocked memories she had hidden away from herself. The couch was where she and Jace made out when no one else was home; the coffee table was where she and Jace had done their homework together. Even the Christmas decorations on the mantle were the same: garlands and red bows strung along the edges. So many things she had left behind.

But Jace was tugging on her hand, leading her through the living room and into the dining room. He slowed to a stop outside the kitchen, just out of sight. His family's voices floated through the doorway, loud, familiar voices, but Selena's heart was pumping too fast to tune into what they were saying. She had told herself that she was coming here for Jace, but as she stood outside the kitchen, ready to walk in, to face them nine years after she left, Selena knew this wasn't just for him.

How many times had she eaten brunch at their table, fell asleep on their couch? While her own parents had been wary of her relationship with Jace, his family had folded her into their lives. Even his mother in her own way. She had made sure she set a place at the table for Selena at Sunday brunch, even toward the end, when she and Jace were falling apart. Had his mother set a place for her today? Selena was too nervous to look now.

"It's going to be fine, Lee," Jace whispered. "You'll see."

She nodded, straightened up, and walked into the kitchen.

Andrew and their mother were standing over a large roast, in the middle of a debate, and Drake, Lizzie, their father and the woman who must be Andrew's fiancé were gathered around them like spectators.

"The thermometer says it's done," said

Andrew.

His mother shook her head. "There's no way it could be done in that little time."

"We can cut it open."

"And lose all the juices?"

Andrew mumbled something she couldn't hear, and then there was a pause. So Selena took a deep breath and stepped forward. "Hi everyone."

She held her breath as they all turned around. Andrew's expression was guarded, and his mother just looked her up and down, assessing. Selena tried to take in each person's reaction, but it wasn't easy. Years ago, she had hurt Jace. Badly. They had every right to be wary, so she just stood in the quiet kitchen, waiting.

Then Jace's father smiled. It was a new version of the way he used to smile at her, the kind of smile that crinkled at the corners of his eyes. "Selena, s-s-sweetheart. Welcome home."

CHAPTER FIFTEEN

Jace watched as his father slowly made his way across his parents' kitchen. The room was quiet aside from his heavy steps and the thump of his cane, but his father was smiling. Selena took a few steps forward, meeting him halfway.

"It's so good to see you," she whispered, and some of the tension in her shoulders eased as his father wrapped his good arm around her.

Jace could see the moment Andrew decided to give Selena a chance. He abandoned the food and led Mary Louise to Selena, hugging and introducing her, and Drake followed right behind. Lizzie hung back behind Drake, his sister's smile tentative but warm. Of all his family, Lizzie had been the closest to Selena, and she had been the most hurt when Selena left without saying goodbye.

He understood that it would take time before they trusted that he and Selena were together for real this time. Hell, they were just starting to build trust between each other. But Jace's family had loved her once. It could take a little time, but she belonged in his family.

His mother... well, that would have to be a work in progress. Wary was the nicest way to characterize her reaction when Jace had told her that he and Selena were rekindling their relationship. But as his mother watched the rest of the family gather around Selena, her sharp gaze was softening.

The rest of the family began to move dishes and drinks to the dining room table, leaving Selena and his mother facing each other. Selena set the gift bag she had brought onto the counter and pulled out a card from it. Her chest rose and fell in a long breath, and then she walked over to his mother.

Jace wanted to follow her, stand next to her and make sure this went well, but it was better for Selena to do this on her own. Instead, he headed for the refrigerator and pretended to look for drinks while he eavesdropped.

"I'm sure you have a lot of questions," said Selena. Her voice was quiet. "I wrote you a card, for later. And if you want to talk, I'd be happy to do that too."

Jace stilled, waiting for his mother's response. Was she going to reject it? Andrew came back in the room, and grabbed the roast off the counter, but his mother didn't even glance in his direction. The kitchen was quiet again, and Jace struggled to get a read on the situation from his not-so-subtle position. As far as he could tell, neither of them had moved.

Finally, his mother reached for the card. "Did you make this?"

Selena nodded, and his mother's expression softened a little. Oh, how he loved this woman, who took the time to learn the road to his prickly mother's heart.

"Thank you. I'll read it." She slipped the card into her pocket, then reached for Selena's cheek, stroking it with her hand. "If you two want a second chance, please use it wisely."

Selena nodded. "That's important to me, too."

Jace let out a sigh. It was a good start.

His mother nodded, then joined the rest of the family as they finished getting the table ready for brunch, so Jace closed the refrigerator door and headed for Selena.

She raised an eyebrow at him. "Did you find what you were looking for in there?"

Jace chuckled as he wrapped his arms around her, kissing her on the temple. "You made my mother a card?"

She nodded. "There's one for Lizzie, too. But I'm waiting for the right time, when we're alone."

"You're amazing," he whispered, relaxing into the warmth of her body.

"You didn't give me a lot of time to prepare, but I think they turned out well." She slipped her hands to his waist.

"I'm guessing it wasn't one of those sexy holiday cards you were working on."

Selena laughed. "Hell, no. It's from an old picture that I found of your parents together on your couch."

"Sounds perfect." He squeezed her closer. "Have I told you I'm falling in love with you all over again?"

"Me, too, Jace," she said. "It's so soon, but it's happening. Like all these feelings were still buried inside me, waiting for you to walk back into my life again."

"I *towed* you back into my life," he corrected her with a smile.

The kitchen was empty, so he bent down and kissed her. It was soft and private, and yet it wasn't about sex. The kiss was like a spell, wrapping around them, connecting them back together. It was full of love, love that Jace had shut down, buried for years, tried to forget. But now with Selena in his arms, the feeling of *them* was both fresh and familiar, both magical and real.

When he pulled back from the kiss, Selena's eyes were dewy with the hint of tears. "I want this, Jace. So badly. All of it. All the things we couldn't give each other nine years ago. We can do it now."

"I want this, too," he said, his voice coming out rough. "We'll get it right this time. But first, let's go into the dining room before anyone comes looking for us."

*

It was late afternoon by the time they turned

down Selena's street, and the snow was falling everywhere. Jace parked in her driveway, and they waded through newly formed drifts to her front porch. The sky was darkening, and white lights glowed from inside the house. Selena stole a glance at Jace, bundled in his winter clothes, his hair messy and his mouth turned up into a hint of a smile. It was still hard to remember that this was real.

In his parents' kitchen, with Jace's arms around her, she had started to believe, really believe they'd get it right this time. She could go to sleep wrapped in Jace's arms and wake up with his big, hard body pressed against hers. Every day. Maybe they could have a loud, fun family of their own, with mini-Jaces running around, or maybe it would just be the two of them, carving out a future together. But for the first time in years, she was ready to dream.

They shuffled inside the house, stomping off the snow from their boots and shedding their winter layers. As Selena hung up her coat, Jace came up behind her. He swept her hair to the side and kissed her neck.

"You're awfully quiet," he whispered.

"Just thinking about us."

"Us naked together, or the future of us?"

Selena turned around and smiled up at him. "Both."

Jace's eyes were bright with happiness. Her heart squeezed in her chest. More than anything, she wanted to be a part of that happiness.

"I want to stay here," she whispered. "Here in Sacred Harbor. I want *us*."

Jace let out a whoop of joy, and then she was off her feet and in his arms, heading up the stairs and down the hall, toward the bedroom. He lay her on the bed and climbed up over her. She slipped her arms around him, pulling him closer, letting everything else fade except for his warm body, pressing against hers. He rested on his elbows and peppered her cheeks and nose and lips with kisses.

"I love you, Selena," he whispered. "I don't think I ever stopped loving you."

She looked into his eyes, giving him the whole, simple truth. "I love you, too."

He was hard against her, but he didn't seem to be in a hurry to get undressed. And neither was she. The dinner with his family, the quiet drive home, with their hands laced together, the snow falling outside the window, covering everything, the feeling of *them*—all of it was magical. She wanted to hold onto this feeling forever.

CHAPTER SIXTEEN
One year later

Jace looked down at the suitcase, lying on the bed in front of him. Most of it was stuffed to the brim, with the exception of a small corner.

"I can't fit all my clothes into that little part of the suitcase," he called through the bathroom door to Selena. "Are you sure the other one is full?"

"It's hot in Mexico, even in December," she called back. "As long as we have our bathing suits and a couple T-shirts, we'll be fine."

He pulled out a few, neatly rolled shirts, new and much too small for either of them. Underneath were books. "What is all this other stuff?"

"Christmas presents. I tried to keep them small, but Lizzie and I went a little crazy at the bookstore in town yesterday."

The bathroom door opened, and Selena walked out, wrapped only in a towel. Her wet hair hung down over her shoulders, and her skin glistened as the steam billowed out, all around her. Jace's heart sped up as she crossed the room. Even after ten months of living together, watching Selena walk through *their* bedroom still left him breathless. He was glad he had insisted on getting new furniture for the house she used to share with another man. Now this beautiful house on the beach felt like their home.

Selena walked straight for him, pressing her body up against his, and she tilted her head up for a kiss. Her lips were so warm and soft from the shower. He pulled her closer, and her kiss turned hungrier, so he stepped back until he found the bed. *Their bed.* She climbed onto his lap, straddling him, laughing. Could she feel the little square box in his pocket? If so, she didn't let on.

"Do we have time for this? We can't miss our plane."

"Two hours before we are supposed to leave from here," he mumbled, kissing her neck.

"We've have been known to spend more time than that in bed." She found the hem of his shirt and slipped her hands under it.

True, but there was something else he wanted to do today before they left, something he had been waiting to do for a while. When he had moved into her house and they had started their lives together, the topic of marriage had come up more than once. Yes, that's what she wanted, and he sure as hell did, too. But those discussions were more about the idea of getting married, not making plans. Was this too soon? Or was the timing perfect?

Today was the start of their holidays together. It was hard to take time off at the shop, but their lead technician was taking over for the next two weeks, and his father was well enough to run the business side. His family had wanted them home for Christmas celebrations, but they understood. He and Selena were getting their first stretch of time together, just for them. The first week in Mexico would be with her family, and the second one was alone on the beach. They'd be newly engaged...hopefully. If she said yes, they'd have two weeks together to celebrate. If she said no, well he'd worry about that when it happened.

Jace tried to slow the pounding of his heart as he gave her one more kiss. "So basically, we'll be taking home an empty suitcase."

She shook her head. "Not a chance. Everyone will have presents for us, too. Especially my parents."

"I got your parents something, but my present doesn't take up half the suitcase."

She tickled him, and he fell back on to the bed, laughing, taking her with him.

Her parents hadn't been at all surprised to hear that he and Selena had gotten back together. They had known how close Selena had come to staying behind with him. And part of him was glad they had pushed her to leave him behind, go to college, and pursue her own path. Especially now that he knew this path led back to him.

Jace was stalling. The ring was in his pocket, the one he had kept all these years in the box with her cards. He had considered getting a new one. Would a new ring be best for their new start? He certainly could afford a more expensive one now. But he'd decided that this second chance should be connected to the first time they fell in love. The truth was his feelings weren't separate from the ones he had had in high school, but they had grown, changed. And these changes let their relationship develop into something new, something stronger.

Selena pulled back a little, her brow furrowed. "You have something on your mind?"

"Just you."

He could hear how serious his voice sounded. Her eyes widened, and her movements slowed. The last time he had asked, he had taken her by surprise. Did she know it was coming this time? If she did, she wasn't running away.

"You're giving me a look," she whispered, "and it's not about having sex."

He nodded solemnly. "You ready for it this time, Lee?"

She blinked her eyes, her dark lashes fluttering. "I am." She lifted her hands to his biceps and squeezed. "You're not just doing this for my parents' sake, are you? So we can sleep in the same room when we get to Mexico?"

Jace's eyes widened. Despite the heavy emotions swirling inside, he laughed. "Would they put us in separate rooms?" He took a moment to process that picture. Not quite the vacation he had imagined. One more reason to do this now.

She was still lying on top of him, so he shifted to his side, their legs tangled and her towel slipping open. And she was smiling, just for him. Jace swallowed. *Focus*. He reached into his pocket and pulled out the box.

"Selena, I loved you many years ago, and I love the woman you are today even more deeply. I want this to be forever. I don't know where this journey will take us. If you decide you want to leave Sacred Harbor, we'll figure that out. I'm willing to give you what you need to make this work, whatever that is, just like you've given me what I need this last year." He took one more deep breath and then said the words. "Will you marry me?"

"Yes, Jace," she said, kissing him. "Yes, yes, yes."

Jace was shaking as he slipped on the ring, but her next kiss steadied him. It was slow and deep and full of certainty.

"Damn," she whispered between kisses. "You waited long enough this time."

He chuckled. "I was ready last December."

"Me too. But if you had asked then, I would've wondered if it was the magic fruitcake talking."

"I wouldn't have wondered, but I'm pretty sure my family would've." Jace tilted his head. "I still can't believe you made your own version of that fruitcake and sent it to Drake's work."

143

A corner of her mouth quirked up mischievously. "Your brother is divorced and all alone in New York. When we went to see him, he seemed a little lonely."

Jace rolled his eyes. "Yeah, all alone in his penthouse suite, rolling in his money."

"Hey, that money is what gave the garage a boost to hire another technician, which is the only reason we have a vacation."

"Ahh, yes," he said. "And now it's our engagement vacation."

This was where they were supposed to be, together. He wrapped his hands around her hips and pulled her closer against him.

Selena reached for the button of his pants. "Now it's time to start this engagement vacation properly."

EPILOGUE

Talk of the Town
By Miss B., Oregon Coastside Patch staff writer

This week's Talk of the Town column is a delicious slice of the holidays from Delilah's Cove. Rumor has it that the sleepy town has been inundated with visitors this December, hoping to get a taste of the holiday magic that put our stretch of the coast on the map.

An anonymous fruitcake that makes people fall in love? Dear reader, this delectable story was too tempting to pass up. I had to get to the bottom of the mystery. After hearing reports that Tuff's Diner had added a fruitcake to the menu, I headed for this potential hotspot for gossip on the subject. Armed with my notebook and dressed inconspicuously, I parked myself at the Tuff's Diner counter and innocently ordered a cup of coffee and the fruitcake. The waitress raised her eyebrow and looked at her watch.

"It's 11:13 a.m., and you're the third order of fruitcake today," she said. "You better hope this batch isn't magical. The last guy who ordered it was at least eighty years old."

When I asked if Tuff's Diner had seen a boom in business since the USA Times article had run in December, she gestured to the bustling restaurant.

"We hired three new servers this December," she said, "but Tuff still isn't happy about the witch rumors."

As I stared at my slice of fruitcake, debating whether or not to taste it, the following Talk of the Town was overheard:

"What happens if I order the whole cake?"

"You can't order that. You're already married."

"I can't believe I'm paying to eat fruitcake."

"How soon do we know if this slice is the real deal?"

The place was bubbling with speculation.

Half-baked publicity stunt or magic? As for Tuff's Diner's version, I'm skeptical. Dear reader, in the spirit of investigation, I tasted my slice of fruitcake. Eighty years old is a little beyond the limits of my dating pool, so what better test of the magic than to try? No swoony octogenarians to report as of this printing.

My question still remains: Who is making the magical fruitcake that continues to put Delilah's Cove on the map? After two hours at Tuff's Diner, I still didn't have anything close to an answer. Now that the holiday season is over, we'll have to wait another year for the next round of anonymous deliveries.

*

THE END

ACKNOWLEDGEMENTS

Writing this book was itself a second chance story. I originally wrote a shorter version of Jace and Selena's romance for the *12 Nights of Christmas* anthology, so my first shout-out goes to the eleven other amazing authors who were a part of that project. A special mention goes to Stacy Finz, both for the first news article that appears in this book and for being my critique partner and unwavering source of support in this crazy career.

Thank you so much to Becca for helping me see so many new possibilities in this story, and thank you to both Kira and my sister Leah for insightful comments. xo.

ABOUT THE AUTHOR

Rebecca Hunter is the award-winning author of sensual, emotional adventures of the heart. She is a reader, traveler, former English teacher, chocolate lover, and keeper of a very messy desk.

Over the years, Rebecca has called many places home, including Michigan, where she grew up, New York City, San Francisco, and Stockholm. After their most recent move from Sweden back to the San Francisco Bay Area, she and her husband assured each other they'll never move again. Well, probably not.

Rebecca's debut book, *Stockholm Diaries, Caroline*, won the 2016 National Excellence in Romance Fiction Award (NERFA), and *Best Laid Plans*, the first book in her Blackmore Inc. series for the Harlequin Dare line, won the 2019 NERFA and the 2019 HOLT Medallion contests and earned a starred review from Library Journal. She's currently writing more super-sexy books for Harlequin Dare...along with a secret project or two.